Peleg Whitman Chandler

Memoir of Governor Andrew

With personal reminiscences: to which are added two hitherto unpublished literary

discourses and the valedictory address

Peleg Whitman Chandler

Memoir of Governor Andrew
With personal reminiscences: to which are added two hitherto unpublished literary discourses and the valedictory address

ISBN/EAN: 9783337092658

Printed in Europe, USA, Canada, Australia, Japan

Cover: Foto ©Raphael Reischuk / pixelio.de

More available books at **www.hansebooks.com**

MEMOIR

OF

GOVERNOR ANDREW,

With Personal Reminiscences.

BY

PELEG W. CHANDLER.

TO WHICH ARE ADDED

Two Hitherto Unpublished Literary Discourses,
and the Valedictory Address.

BOSTON:
ROBERTS BROTHERS.
1880.

PUBLISHERS' NOTICE.

THIS Memoir of GOVERNOR ANDREW was prepared at the request of the Massachusetts Historical Society and appeared in their Proceedings for April, 1880. The publishers have obtained consent to re-print it, and the author has, at their solicitation, added some personal reminiscences. They have also inserted two literary discourses of the Governor which have never been published, for the manuscripts of which they are indebted to the courtesy of his eldest son, John Forrester Andrew, Esq.

OCTOBER, 1880.

PREFACE.

Immediately after the death of Governor Andrew, in 1868, the Massachusetts Historical Society took appropriate action, and a member was appointed to prepare a Memoir of our deceased Associate. The unusual delay in this work has arisen partly from the authoritative announcement that an accomplished writer was collecting materials for an extended biography of the great War Governor, and it seemed best to postpone the sketch for this Society in the hope of being able to make a more satisfactory statement of Mr. Andrew's life and labors, from the light thrown upon them by a biographer selected by the family, one in every way competent to the work. It is now probable that the Memoir referred to will not be published for a considerable time, if at all. Moreover, at the time of Mr. Andrew's death the fires of controversy were still burning, and it was thought that the subject might be treated in a more just and dispassionate way after the lapse of time, when the principles on which he acted could be better appreciated and the prophetic character of his writings might be tested by time and experience. There was also a natural reluctance on the part of one of his earliest and most constant friends to attempt, in the space usually allowed for matters of this kind, the analysis of a character so remarkable, which should be just to him and loyal to the truth. In the Uffizi Gallery at Florence there is a remarkable bust of Brutus, left unfinished by Michael Angelo. An English scholar explains the fact in some lines indicating that the artist abandoned his labor in despair, because overcome by the grandeur of the subject : —

> "Brutum efficisset sculptor, sed mente recursat
> Tanta viri virtus, sistit, et obstupuit."

It is with something of this feeling that the sketch just now prepared is submitted to the Society.

CONTENTS.

LIST OF ILLUSTRATIONS.

MEMOIR.

MEMOIR.

John Albion Andrew, the twenty-first Governor of Massachusetts, was born at Windham, a small town near Portland, in the State of Maine, May 31, 1818. The family descended from Robert Andrew, who came from England to Rowley Village, now Boxford, and died there in 1688. A grandmother of Governor Andrew was the granddaughter of the famous Captain William Pickering, and the mother of her husband was Mary Higginson, a descendant of Francis Higginson. His grandfather was originally a silversmith, and afterward a merchant in Salem, where his son Jonathan, the Governor's father, was born in 1782. The latter was educated in the public schools and became a trader.

He left Salem in early manhood for Windham, where he bought a small house, still standing, near the Presumpscot River, and established the business of a general trader, in which he was fairly well successful.   He was greatly respected as a citizen, a deacon of the church, a man of substance and of great influence.   In 1817 he married, under interesting circumstances, Miss Nancy Green Pierce, of New Hampshire, who was a teacher in the celebrated academy at Fryeburg, where Daniel Webster was once employed in the same capacity She was thrown from a horse, and was taken to a tavern in Naples where young Andrew happened to be.   An acquaintance there formed resulted in marriage.

Both of these young people were above the ordinary mark.   Jonathan Andrew was a quiet, reticent man, of much intelligence and a keen perception of the ludicrous.   Firm, courageous and resolute, he was at the same time shy, and so unobtrusive as to pass for less than his worth, except to those who knew him well. Of his wife it is almost impossible to speak in terms of exaggeration. She was well educated, with great sweetness of temper, and altogether highly prepossessing in appearance. They had four children, all of whom are now living, except the oldest, — John Albion, born May 31, 1818; Isaac Watson, born Aug 11, 1819; Sarah Elizabeth, born September 6, 1822; Nancy Alfreda, born May 21, 1824.

There never was a more united and happy family. The father possessed ample means for their education, and left his household to the good management of his wife, who was admirable in her domestic arrangements, judicious, sensible, energetic, and a rigid disciplinarian of her children. There was a rare union of gentleness and force in this woman, which made her generally attractive, and especially endeared her to all who came under the influence of her character.

> " Her voice was ever soft,
> Gentle and low, — an excellent thing in woman."

She was a fine singer, and had remarkable conversational powers.[1] Their home was the usual resort of the ministers when visiting or journeying through the town, and in this way the family had excellent opportunities for acquiring information from the cultured men of the day. Mr. Andrew disliked to send his children to the public school, but built a schoolhouse on his own land. Mrs. Andrew, who had been in feeble health for several years, died on the 7th of March, 1832, aged 48. It was a great shock to her husband, who never afterward took much interest in business affairs. He

---

[1] Mr. Andrew, being naturally quite taciturn, always desired his wife to lead off in conversation. The Governor used to tell with great glee a story which illustrated their different characteristics. The deacon, like all the country traders of that day, dealt in ardent spirits. When the temperance reform was started, his wife entered into it with great interest. She was particularly desirous that he should give up the sale of liquor. For weeks, the children used to hear her, after retiring, lecture their father on the subject with earnest volubility. He kept silent; but at length, one night after a discourse of unusual length and vivacity, told her quietly that he had given up the sale for some months.

soon sold out his property in Windham, and removed to a farm in Boxford, in the county where he was born. He died in September, 1849, at the age of 67.[1]

His oldest son was fitted for college at Gorham Academy, then under the charge of a celebrated teacher, the Rev. Reuben Nason. He entered Bowdoin College, in 1833, where his career was in no way remarkable. He is remembered as a bright, genial boy, of curly hair and a somewhat peculiar appearance, short, very thick, and his head and body out of proportion to the lower extremities. He was not adapted to the ordinary college sports, in which he appeared to take very little interest. As a

[1] Jonathan Andrew was devotedly attached to his children ; but, like all shy and taciturn men, he was grave in appearance, and his children had something of the old-fashioned awe and respect in their intercourse with him. In the only letter to him from the Governor which is preserved (1844), he is addressed as " Honored Father," and the signature is " Your dutiful son." The first letter John A. Andrew wrote to his father in college was addressed " Dear Father," and signed, " Yours affectionately." The father sent him word that this was not proper, but that his letters should be addressed as above.

scholar he was among the lowest in the class; he took no part at Commencement. But he was by no means an idler. On the contrary he was constantly occupied in general reading, greatly interested in current literature, and always ready for discussion, especially of political topics. He was popular among all without any effort to be so, and always so genial, without the least self-consciousness, as to render him an unusual favorite. He was not regarded as dull, very much the contrary; but he seemed to be indifferent to the ordinary routine of college honors — possessed of that happy temperament which enabled him then and for many years afterward to pass quietly along without a touch of the emulous jealousies and temptations that wait on the ambitious aspirations of the young as well as the old.

On coming to Boston, he entered the office of the late Henry H. Fuller, with whom he passed his whole novitiate. It always seemed to me that his character

was much affected by contact with that
somewhat remarkable and much misunderstood lawyer. Mr. Fuller was a man of
genial temperament, an excellent scholar
(second in the class of which Edward
Everett was first), of wide reading and extensive acquirements, — a man who loved
young men and assisted them in every
way he could; and also of such marked
peculiarities, of such wonderful crotchets
and such heroic obstinacy, that he naturally and especially attracted, and, in some
respects, almost fascinated his pupil. The
attraction between him and young Andrew
was mutual. They became almost like
brothers. The student sat at the same
desk with the master, entered into all the
business affairs of the office, wrote letters
from dictation, and was consulted on almost
every subject that came up; so that they
seemed, in fact, like one person. Mr. Fuller had an extensive acquaintance with all
sorts of men. He knew the personal history of almost every citizen of the town

and of all public characters, living and
dead. He had decided opinions, which
he never hesitated to pronounce on any
suitable occasion. Mr. Andrew, with the
curiosity of a young man fresh from the
country, took this all in; but what is remarkable, while some of the peculiar traits
of the master stuck to the pupil, the latter
had decided opinions of his own, especially
in regard to American slavery, which were
sometimes in ludicrous contrast with those
of his senior. Mr. Fuller was a conservative of conservatives. He stood by the
ancient ways even in the cut of his coat
and the shape of his hat; his ruffled shirt,
his white cravat, shirt-collar, and tall bell-
crowned hat of real fur, were significant of
a past generation. Young Andrew became
interested in many of the reform move-
ments of the day, and was as firm and
peculiar in one direction as his friend was
in another.

He did not rise rapidly at the bar. He
was a faithful and painstaking lawyer, look-

ing up his cases with care and industry, and probably never lost a client who had once employed him. Here, too, he always seemed destitute of ambition — that is, in the ordinary meaning of the term. He did his duty and there was an end. It has been said that he was not a learned lawyer. Perhaps in one sense he was not; he certainly was not a legal pedant. There are men who study for the profession with great patience and perseverance, who master in the outset its main principles and are thoroughly prepared, so far as books are concerned, for whatever may come. They are veterans almost before they have seen service. There are other men who, from the force of circumstances or their mental characteristics, have not carefully read all the text-books, and are obliged, after coming to the bar, to pick up their law as they need it, — raw recruits who will become veterans by actual service, unless picked off in some battle at an early and unexpected stage of their practice. By studying their cases, investigating every collateral point and going to the bottom of the matter, they are enabled to master the present difficulties, and, in the course of time, become able and even learned lawyers, without the reputation of being so from the fact of early deficiencies.

Mr. Andrew entered upon the investigation of his cases with great zeal and industry. No man at the bar studied harder. When he tried a cause he meant to gain it if he could. There was no sentimentalism here. He used any proper weapon he could find in the armory of the law; and he liked success even on the most technical points. He tried a case with courage, perseverance, spirit, and a dash of old-fashioned but manly temper. Those who have been associated with or opposed to him in the courts know very well that he was a dangerous opponent long before he had much reputation as a lawyer.

During all these years he was not what is called a student, but was never idle. He

entered largely into many of the moral
questions of that day; was greatly interested in the preaching of James Freeman Clarke; a constant attendant at meetings and the Bible classes. Occasional lay
preaching being the custom of that church,
young Andrew sometimes occupied the
pulpit and conducted the services to the
general acceptance of the people.

His personal qualities were most attractive. Those who admired him at a distance loved him on acquaintance. It is
difficult for people who did not know him
intimately to appreciate or even to understand the personal magnetism of this man.
His respectful deference towards the sex
was conspicuous, his love of children intense; and there was such an entire simplicity, unpretending geniality, united to
fun and drollery, as to attract everybody
to him. Everywhere and at all times he
was welcome. He was fond of music.
Although without scientific knowledge,
he had a good voice and sang with great

spirit, especially in the old ballads and hymns. It was worth a journey to hear him in Coronation or Dundee, Tamworth or Old Hundred. He was an excellent reader, and was always willing to delight the circle by a repetition of old ballads, or the reading of poems, particularly of Gray's Elegy.

He was full of wit and anecdote — brimful; not merely of the sort which is found in books and newspapers, or which floats in polite society. In stores and taverns, in stage-coaches, among the laborers of the corn-field and in haying-time, he had heard the Yankee dialect with all its wit and humor, and he never forgot any thing, especially if it were droll. In his knowledge and appreciation of New England character, of the town system, and of the laws affecting municipal corporations, he greatly resembled the late Chief Justice Shaw, — that great magistrate whose grim appearance on the bench gave no token of the warm heart and genial nature he

actually had, and the love of fun and anecdote which was conspicuous in the social
circle, and especially at the Law and Fri-
day Clubs.

At the same time, Governor Andrew,
although so mirthful and even boyish in
social life and in business affairs, was, as the
chief executive officer of the Commonwealth,
a great stickler for proper forms and ceremonies. It was also quite noticeable that in
his public speeches he seldom indulged in
a humorous strain, or told a story to illustrate a point in his argument. It is not
improbable, that, while he gained something in dignity, there was a loss in interest and in the power of illustration, which
is possessed by those who are capable of
applying homely maxims or humorous stories to argumentative discourse. Illustration is to logic sometimes what concussion
is to pressure in mechanics. The blow of a
mallet may drive in a wedge more effectually than the weight of many tons.

On his admission to the bar Governor

Andrew became active in politics, an energetic and enthusiastic member of the Whig party, often speaking " on the stump," and thoroughly in earnest.   Of his interest in the anti-slavery movement, it is necessary to speak a little more at length.

From early youth, Andrew was interested in all questions affecting the happiness of the race.   At thirteen, he made a speech in a public meeting at Windham, on temperance.   While in college, he was constantly discussing the anti-slavery question: and it was at this time (1833) that he sent a work of Mrs. L. M. Child, entitled " An Appeal in favor of that class of Americans called Africans," to his sisters, with these words written on the fly-leaf: —

" To my two sisters this little volume is affectionately presented, with the fervent aspiration that the instruction contained in it, and inculcated by one of the gifted ones of their own sex, may prompt their hearts to pity for the oppressed African, may uproot all prejudice that may be implanted there against those immortal beings, whose only crime is that of being unfortunate

To my two Sisters this little volume is affectionately presented with the fervent aspiration that the instruction contained in it, and inculcated by one of the gifted ones of their own sex, may prompt their hearts to pity for the oppressed African, may uproot all prejudice that may be implanted them against those immortal beings, whose only crime is that of being unfortunate and having a skin of a darker hue than their own, and may teach them to remember that of one blood God made all the nations of the earth. Your brother

Albion

and having a skin of a darker hue than their own, and may teach them to remember that ' of one blood God made all the nations of the earth.'

" Your Brother,

" ALBION."

In 1859, he was a member of the lower branch of the Legislature, and at once took a prominent and leading position. In 1860, he was nominated for Governor of the Commonwealth, " by a genuine popular impulse which overwhelmed the old political managers, who regarded him as an intruder upon the arena, and had laid other plans. " When he was nominated as Governor, there were many who voted for him with hesitation, in the fear that a man so radical, so firm and so outspoken, might be unsafe in action. His friends, whether agreeing with him or not, judged him better. They knew his practical sense, and felt sure that whatever rhetorical expressions might have escaped his lips, his action would be safe. Even they were disappointed, however, in the immense executive ability he displayed from the first hour he entered the State House until he left it. The simplicity and directness of his action as Chief Magistrate were as remarkable as they were sometimes amusing. He never was deterred by provincial conventionalisms from doing what he thought right, and in the way he deemed best. Formalism or snobbery or red tape never stood in his way a moment. He was a keen observer and understood all the proprieties of his position perfectly well. No one was likely to impose upon him by mere manner, and, while he never intentionally gave offence, it was obvious that he understood the character of men very well, whatever might be their style or dress. He found no difficulty in discerning merit, although covered with rags, and a black skin did not alarm him. Indeed, the adverse personal surroundings of men that usually operate against them had precisely the opposite effect on him; and he was sometimes imposed upon by this very fact.

It is hardly necessary to say, that, at no period since the adoption of the constitution was the position of Chief Magistrate of Massachusetts so arduous and responsible as at the time of his accession to the office. But he was found equal to the emergency, and early acquired, by general consent, the title of "the great War Governor." This is not the place for any thing more than a general statement of what he did. Nor is it consistent with the usages of this Society to enter into a discussion of controverted political points, in connection with biographical sketches of our deceased associates.

In his inaugural address (1861), he advised that a portion of the militia should be placed on a footing of activity, in order that "in the possible contingencies of the future, the State might be ready, without inconvenient delay, to contribute her share of force in any exigency of public danger "; and immediately upon being inducted into office, he despatched a confidential messenger to the Governors of Maine and New Hampshire, to inform them of his determination to prepare for instant service the militia of Massachusetts, and to invite their co-operation. His military orders and purchases of war material subjected him to much ridicule and reproach, but subsequent events fully justified his course, and his acts were looked upon as evidence of remarkable foresight. The quiet opposition at the time, however, in the Legislature was very strong, and it came in considerable part from his own political friends. Indeed it is a remarkable fact, that while an unquestionable majority of the people were in his favor, a majority of the Legislature was really opposed to him, although not venturing upon any direct collision. A leading member of the House and of the party, at the session of 1862, told me that Governor Andrew ought never again to be a candidate for the office of governor; that his re-election was impossible. His ways were not the ways of politicians; his methods were not their methods, and he did not count much on their support, or fear the opposition of those who were governed by ideas of mere expediency in emergencies involving principles, and requiring the earnest efforts and unselfish devotion of men who hoped for ultimate success by a firm reliance on truth and justice. He looked with something like contempt and even abhorrence upon all makeshift attempts at compromise, where the great interests of humanity were to be sacrificed to the pressing emergencies which are the refuge and final destruction of the weak and cowardly.

He was chosen governor in 1860 and retired from office at the end of 1865. These were years of unexampled interest and importance in the history of the country. It soon became clear that the Governor was remarkably well fitted for the new and trying duties of the position. Those who knew him best were of the opinion that, in the ordinary and peaceful administration of affairs he might never have shown the remarkable ability which he possessed; and some even maintained that, although he could scarcely have made a failure, he might have passed into history with the crowd of high officials who perform their duties fairly well, but attain no marked prominence in the history and progress of human affairs.

In this man, however, there was a rare union of intellectual ability, enthusiasm, firmness, unflinching courage and undoubting religious faith, which enabled him to meet every trying emergency as it arose, to surmount unexpected difficulties, and to inspire in all who watched him an admiration that encouraged while it sustained their own efforts in the defence of the great principles on which our government rests.

It is impossible in this brief sketch to go into much detail as to the Governor's services in these memorable years, but an allusion to some of the prominent points may be expected.[1] The alacrity with which he met the call of the President for troops, and the energy displayed in sending off the first regiments are well remembered. From the first moment that it became clear there was to be war, he entered into the campaign with all the ardor of his nature. " Immediately," he wrote to President Lincoln, on the 3d of May, " on receiving your Proclamation, we took up the war, and have carried on our part of it, in the spirit in which we believe the Administration and the American people intend to act, namely, as if there was not an inch of red tape in the world."

He early saw the weakest point of the Confederates, and constantly maintained that a blow should be struck at the institu-

[1] There are in the State House of this Commonwealth more than thirty thousand pages of letters relating to the war, and Governor Andrew's private correspondence occupies some five thousand pages more. Any adequate account of his services can be given only by a complete history of the Civil War. During his administration he sent to the two branches of the Legislature nearly one hundred messages.

tion which lay at the foundation of all our troubles, by calling the negroes of the South to rally in defence of the flag. Others had doubts, others hesitated, but his vision was clear from the start, and he never wavered.   When the first colored regiment was formed, he remarked to a friend, that, in regard to other regiments, he accepted men as officers who were sometimes rough and uncultivated, "but these men," he said, " shall be commanded by officers who are eminently and technically *gentlemen*."

It was in January, 1863, that official sanction was given to the raising of colored troops.   The Governor obtained in a personal interview with the Secretary of War, authority to raise volunteer companies of artillery for duty in the forts of Massachusetts and elsewhere, and such companies of infantry for the volunteer military service as he might find convenient.   To this the Governor added with his own hand the words, "and may include persons of African descent organized into separate corps," to which the Secretary assented. This was the first authorization of an act which caused the greatest excitement everywhere, and struck a heavier blow at the enemy than any before given. One bright May morning the 54th, the equal of the best in the quality, discipline and equipment of the men and the character of the officers, marched down Beacon Street and passed the Governor in review, in presence of fifty thousand men.[1]

In regard to the emancipation of the slaves, Governor Andrew was among the first, as he was the most persistent advocate of a measure which he considered the greatest blow that could be struck at the enemy, fully justified as a measure of war, and demanded by every consideration of justice and humanity. On this subject he manifested more impatience than on any other, and was greatly discouraged, dis-

[1] Sketch of the Military Life of Governor Andrew, by Colonel Albert G. Browne, Jr., military secretary to the Governor.

turbed, and even disgusted by the delays
at Washington, and the obstructions thrown
in the way by those in authority. All this
is matter of history; but an incident occurred in relation to it, which, so far as I
know, has never been in print, and is worth
being stated in connection with this subject, as it is significant in more respects
than one.

Among the Governor's friends was a
young merchant of Boston, and I will let
him tell the story in his own way:—

"It was in the summer of 1862, when
emancipation was being talked a great deal.
We had not had any great successes, and
everybody had a notion that emancipation
ought to come. One day the Governor
sent for me to come up to the State House.
I went up to his room, and I never shall
forget how I met him. He was signing
some kind of bonds, standing at a tall desk
in the council chamber, in his shirt sleeves,
his fingers all covered with ink. He said,
' How do you do? I want you to go to

Washington.' 'Why, Governor,' said I, ' I can 't go to Washington on any such notice as this.   I am busy, and it is impossible for me to go.' 'All my folks are serving their country,' said he ; and he mentioned the various services the members of his staff were engaged in, and said with emphasis, 'Somebody must go to Washington.' 'Well, Governor, I don 't see how I can.' Said he ' I command you to go.' 'Well,' said I, ' Governor, put it in that way and I shall go, of course.' 'There is something going on,' he remarked. 'This is a momentous time.' He turned suddenly toward me and said, 'You believe in prayer, don 't you ? ' I said, 'Why, of course.'   'Then let us pray '; and he knelt right down at the chair that was placed there ; we both kneeled down, and I never heard such a prayer in all my life.   I never was so near the throne of God, except when my mother died, as I was then.   I said to the Governor, ' I am profoundly impressed ; and I will start this afternoon for Washington.'   I soon found

out that emancipation was in everybody's
mouth, and when I got to Washington and
called upon Sumner, he began to talk
emancipation.   He asked me to go and see
the President, and tell him how the people
of Boston and New England regarded it.
I went to the White House that evening
and met the President.   We first talked
about every thing but emancipation, and
finally he asked me what I thought about
emancipation.   I told him what I thought
about it, and said that Governor Andrew
was so far interested in it that I had no
doubt he had sent me on there to post the
President in regard to what the class of
people I met in Boston and New York
thought of it, and then I repeated to him,
as I had previously to Sumner, this prayer
of the Governor's, as well as I could remember it.   The President said, 'When we
have the Governor of Massachusetts to
send us troops in the way he has, and when
we have him to utter such prayers for us, I
have no doubt that we shall succeed.'   In

September the Governor sent for me. He had a despatch that emancipation would be proclaimed, and it was done the next day. You remember the President made proclamation in September to take effect in January. Well, he and I were together alone again in the council-chamber. Said he, 'You remember when I wanted you to go on to Washington?' I said, 'Yes, I remember it very well.' 'Well,' said he, 'I did n't know exactly what I wanted you to go for then. Now I will tell you what let 's do: you sing Coronation, and I 'll join with you.' So we sang together the old tune, and also Praise God from Whom All Blessings Flow. Then I sang Old John Brown, he marching around the room and joining in the chorus after each verse."

It is proper to say here with emphasis, that, although Governor Andrew was occupied during his whole term with national affairs, to an extent altogether unusual in Massachusetts, local interests of the Commonwealth were by no means neglected.

On the contrary, he exercised a careful supervision over all the institutions that had claims upon his time; and was vigilant in seeing that the laws were promptly executed. He frequently visited the various punitory and charitable establishments, and devoted much time to the examination of all special cases where there were questions in regard to pardons or commutations of sentence. Although strongly opposed to capital punishment, he did not hesitate to sign the death-warrant in cases where there were no special reasons for dispensing with the extreme penalty of the law. A glance at his various messages to the Legislature will show that, although denominated a "War Governor," he was by no means inattentive to the ordinary duties of his office.

The first message of the Governor (Jan. 5, 1861) was largely occupied in a discussion of domestic affairs, — the finances of the Commonwealth, Valuation, Agriculture, Banks and Banking, the Usury Laws (earnestly advocating a change), Mutual Insurance Companies, Public Charitable Institutions, Capital Punishment, Practical Scientific Institutions, Boston Harbor and Back Bay, Marriage and Divorce, Cape Cod Canal, the Provincial Statutes, the Two Years' Amendment, the General Statutes, the provisions of the statutes concerning Personal Liberty, the Pacific Railroad.

All of these topics were ably treated. He made a powerful argument against that provision of our law preventing the marriage of a person against whom a decree of divorce had been granted. " This anomaly," he said, " originated many years ago, in certain ecclesiastical theories concerning the institution of marriage, and was devised by the ecclesiastics themselves. In our own age, the theory upon which the law enforces the celibacy of a divorced husband or wife is that of punishment for the offence which was the occasion of the divorce." He recommended a change, so that a power could be lodged in some tribunal to mitigate the hardships of the law, according to the circumstances of each case, whatever may have been the cause of the dissolution of the marriage.

A bill was introduced in accordance with this suggestion, but it met with most violent opposition, especially from clergymen in the House of Representatives, and was defeated. At the next session the Governor again referred to the subject, and renewed his recommendation " for such a modification of our laws touching marriage and divorce as shall lodge in some tribunal the power to mitigate the penalty of celibacy as a consequence of divorce, whatever may have been the cause of the dissolution of the marriage." It was not, however, until 1864 that an act was passed, conferring power on the Supreme Judicial Court to authorize a party against whom a divorce from the bonds of matrimony, for the cause of adultery, had been granted (except where the party had been convicted of adultery) to marry again. (Acts of 1864, ch. 216.)

The Governor, in his message (1861), called attention to the propriety of making some change in the usury laws. He alluded to the fact that, in the year 1818, a very able committee, appointed by the British House of Commons, made an elaborate report recommending a modification of the usury laws. But so strongly were the people opposed to the measure, that more than twenty years elapsed before any favorable action to that end was adopted. At last, in 1839, a law was enacted by Parliament, exempting bills of exchange and promissory notes, not having more than twelve months to run, from the operation of these laws; and for twenty-one years this enactment had been satisfactory to the British public. He suggested whether a similar change in our own laws might not be wise. Nothing was accomplished at that session, but in 1867 the law in Massachusetts was altered to a greater extent than had been recommended by Governor Andrew.

Governor Andrew was strongly opposed to capital punishment and recommended an alteration of the law in his first message. But, as before remarked, he did not allow his convictions on this subject to interfere with the execution of the law while it was in force, and signed the death-warrant in several cases during his term of office.

In his second message (1862) he suggested the expediency of no longer insisting by statute that each Representative in Congress shall be an inhabitant of the district from which he is elected, declaring such a law to be unconstitutional.

When a bill was reported in the House of Representatives to divide the Commonwealth into legislative districts for the choice of Representatives, there was an exciting discussion. Mr. Caleb Cushing and Mr. P. W. Chandler, advocated the course recommended by the Governor, contending that the restrictive clause was clearly unconstitutional, but the act was passed with a clause requiring the people of each Congressional district to limit their choice of Representatives in Congress to an inhabitant of the district. The Governor vetoed the bill in a message containing a masterly argument against its constitutionality and expediency. The act was passed over the veto and is now in operation or rather is *unrepealed*, but has been practically disregarded in several instances.

The message of 1863 was naturally and necessarily much taken up with matters connected with the war, but the economical and other special interests of the Commonwealth received careful attention. The Harbors and Flats, the Troy and Greenfield Railroad, Banking and Currency, Pleuro-Pneumonia, Farming, Public Schools, were sensibly considered. There was also an elaborate discussion of the acts of the 37th Congress granting to each of the several States a portion of the public domain, " to the endowment, support, and maintenance of at least one college, where the

leading object shall be, without excluding
other scientific and classical studies, and
including military tactics, to teach such
branches of learning as are related to agriculture and the mechanic arts in such manner as the Legislatures of the States may
respectively prescribe, in order to promote
the liberal and practical education of the
industrial classes in the several pursuits
and professions in life." The apportionment to each State was, in quantity, equal
to 30,000 acres of land for each Senator
and Representative in Congress, to which
the States were respectively entitled by the
apportionment under the census of 1860.
The Governor entered upon an elaborate
examination of the whole subject, in which
he expressed the opinion that the Congressional grant was exposed to the danger of
being divided in each State among several unimportant seminaries instead of
being concentrated on one institution of
commanding influence and efficiency : —

"The Act of Congress does not make provision sufficient for an Agricultural School of the highest class in each State. Nor would it be possible now to find, disconnected from our colleges and universities, as many men of high talent, and otherwise competent, as would be required to fill the chairs of one such school. But Massachusetts already has in the projected Bussey Institution an agricultural school founded, though not yet in operation, with a large endowment, connected also with Harvard College and the Lawrence Scientific School. She can, therefore, by securing the grant from Congress, combining with the Institute of Technology and the Zoölogical Museum, and working in harmony with the College, secure also for the agricultural student for whom she thus provides, not only the benefits of the national appropriation, but of the Bussey Institution and the means and instrumentalities of the Institute of Technology, as well as those accumulated at Cambridge. The benefits to our State and to our country and to mankind, which can be obtained by this co-operation, are of the highest character, and can be obtained in no other way. The details of the connection of the Bussey Institution with the Scientific School and the College are not yet fully wrought out, but I apprehend that little difficulty would be found in connecting it also with the grant from

Congress, if the gentlemen who may be intrusted by the State with the work will approach it with the perception of the absolute necessity for husbanding our materials, both men and money, and concentrating all our efforts upon making an institution worthy of our age and of our people. Its summit must reach the highest level of modern science, and its heads must be those whom men will recognize as capable of planning a great work, and of working out a great plan."

The message of 1864 was considerably occupied by a consideration of local subjects affecting the special interests of the Commonwealth, all of which were discussed with an ability and discrimination which showed that they had been carefully examined. He recommends the establishment of a military academy, and re-asserts his opinion, expressed the year before in connection with an agricultural college, that, " the one great and commanding duty and capability of our Commonwealth — her way to unchallenged influence and admiration among the States — is the discovering, unfolding, and teaching the secrets of knowledge and their scientific application to the arts of civilized humanity."

The recommendation of Governor Andrew in regard to the Agricultural College was not acceded to by the General Court, and he thus alludes to the subject in the annual message of 1865 :—

"Although overruled by the better judgment of the Legislature as to the views which I had the honor to present at length in the annual address of 1863, and although I remain more fully convinced than ever, after the reflection of two intervening years, of their substantial soundness, I have felt it to be my official duty cordially to co-operate in endeavoring to give vitality and efficient action to the college under the auspices determined by the law of its creation. Of all the places offered and possible under the charter, the place selected by the Trustees seemed justly to be preferred, having in view all the relative advantages of each.

"My own idea of a college likely to be useful in the largest way to the people, most vigorous in its growth, promotive of the progress of thrifty and intelligent farming, productive of scientific and exact knowledge (which is the true basis of prosperity), worthy of Massachusetts, and able to command the respect, while it challenges the pride, of her agricultural community, — is one perhaps not yet to be realized."

Whether the course recommended by the Governor, or the one actually adopted for the establishment of an agricultural college, was the best, there is at this day, in the light of the experience we have had, very little doubt.

While in office Governor Andrew felt obliged to send in no less than twelve veto messages. In ten of these the bills did not pass over his veto. Of the two bills that were passed notwithstanding his veto, one was a Resolve authorizing additional compensation to members of the Legislature. The other was an Act to divide the Commonwealth into districts for the choice of Representatives in the Congress of the United States, to which reference has been made already, which passed the Senate (1862), notwithstanding his veto, by a vote of 22 to 11, and the House by a vote of

137 to 67. It is without doubt unconstitutional in some of its provisions and they have been in fact disregarded.

Governor Andrew's character as a man of practical sense was somewhat misunderstood before his election, and even now the error is not entirely cleared, except to those who carefully watched his official acts. When a distinguished judge expressed some alarm at his nomination for fear of his eccentricities, one who knew him well replied, " Yes; he is an emotional man and a rhetorician; he may have made some extravagant remarks, but did any one ever know him to *do* a foolish thing?" In point of fact he was one of the most sensible, practical and safe governors we ever had. He showed great sagacity and ability in the treatment of business questions where the interests of the Commonwealth were affected, and his recommendations in regard to all matters relating to social science and the economical welfare of the people were discriminating, sound and just. And so in regard to political questions. He was an anti-slavery man from principle. He was thoroughly in earnest in his opposition to the extension of the slave power. While acting with the Whig party of Massachusetts, he never went beyond the line authorized by regular resolutions of that party adopted time and again.

In the course of a long discussion of the provisions of the statutes concerning personal liberty, in his inaugural address of 1861 he says, " In dismissing this topic, I have only to add that, in regard not only to one, but to every subject bearing on her Federal relations, Massachusetts has always conformed to her honest understanding of all constitutional obligations — that she has always conformed to the judicial decisions — has never threatened either to nullify or to disobey — and that the decision in one suit fully contested, constitutes a precedent for the future."

And further on, while speaking of the state of the country, and condemning in severe terms the course of President Buchanan and of some of the Southern States, he says, " And yet, during all the excitement of this period, inflamed by the heats of repeated Presidential elections, I have never known a single Massachusetts Republican to abandon his loyalty, surrender his faith, or seal up his heart against the good hopes and kind affections which every devoted citizen ought to entertain for every section of his country. During all this mal-administration of the national government, the people of Massachusetts have never wavered from their faith in its principles or their loyalty to its organization."

But he fully comprehended at that early time the momentous issue involved, which was, more than the union of these States, even the very existence of a republican government in any country.

" Upon this issue over the heads of all mere politicians and partisans, in behalf of the Commonwealth of Massachusetts, I appeal directly to the warm hearts and clear heads of the great masses of the people. The men who own and till the soil, who drive the mills, and hammer out their own iron and leather on their own anvils and lap-stones, and they who, whether in the city or the country, reap the rewards of enterprising industry and skill in the varied pursuits of business, are honest, intelligent, patriotic, independent, and brave. They know that simple defeat in an election is no cause for the disruption of a government. They know that those who declare that they will not live peaceably within the Union do not mean to live peaceably out of it. They know that the people of all sections have a right, which they intend to maintain, of free access from the interior to both oceans, and from Canada to the Gulf of Mexico, and of the free use of all the lakes and rivers and highways of commerce, North, South, East, or West. They know that the Union means peace, and unfettered commercial intercourse from sea to sea and from shore to shore ; that it secures us all against the unfriendly presence or possible dictation of any foreign power, and commands respect for our flag and security for our trade. And they do not intend, nor will they ever consent, to be excluded from these rights which they have so long enjoyed, nor to abandon the prospect of the benefits which Humanity claims for itself by means of their continued enjoyment in the future.

Neither will they consent that the continent shall be overrun by the victims of a remorseless cupidity, and the elements of civil danger increased by the barbarizing influences which accompany the African slave-trade. Inspired by the same ideas and emotions which commanded the fraternization of Jackson and Webster on another great occasion of public danger, the people of Massachusetts, confiding in the patriotism of their brethren in other States, accept this issue, and respond, in the words of Jackson, ' *The Federal Union, it must be preserved.'* "

After the die was cast, he urged a vigorous prosecution of the war and insisted on every measure to defeat the Confederate armies that was consistent with the laws of war. He was particularly strenuous in demanding the emancipation of the slaves. On this point, I cannot do better than to quote from the admirable sketch of the Governor by his military secretary during the war, Albert G. Browne, Jr., Esq.

" Over the bodies of our soldiers who were killed at Baltimore he had recorded a prayer that he might live to see the end of the war, and a

vow that, so long as he should govern Massachusetts, and so far as Massachusetts could control
the issue, it should not end without freeing every
slave in America. He believed, at the first, in
the policy of emancipation as a war measure.
Finding that timid counsels controlled the government at Washington, and the then commander
of the Army of the Potomac, so that there was
no light in that quarter, he hailed the action of
Frémont in Missouri in proclaiming freedom to
the western slaves. Through all the reverses
which afterwards befell that officer he never
varied from this friendship; and when at last
Frémont retired from the Army of Virginia, the
Governor offered him the command of a Massachusetts regiment, and vainly urged him to take
the field again under our State flag. Just so,
afterwards, he welcomed the similar action of
Hunter in South Carolina, and wrote in his defence the famous letter in which he urged, ' to
fire at the enemy's magazine.' He was deeply
disappointed when the Administration disavowed
Hunter's act, for he had hoped much from the
personal friendship which was known to exist
between the General and the President. Soon
followed the great reverses of McClellan before
Richmond.

"The feelings of the Governor at this time on
the subject of emancipation are well expressed

in a speech which he made on Aug. 10, 1862, at
the Methodist camp meeting on Martha's Vine-
yard. It was the same speech in which occurs
his remark, since so often quoted: —

" ' I know not what record of sin awaits me in
the other world, but this I know, that I was never
mean enough to despise any man because he was
ignorant, or because he was poor, or because he
was black.'

" Referring to slavery, he said : —

" ' I have never believed it to be possible that
this controversy should end, and peace resume
her sway, until that dreadful iniquity has been
trodden beneath our feet. I believe it cannot,
and I have noticed, my friends (although I am
not superstitious, I believe), that, from the day
our government turned its back on the proclamation of General Hunter, the blessing of God has
been withdrawn from our arms. We were marching on, conquering and to conquer ; post after
post had fallen before our victorious arms ; but
since that day I have seen no such victories.
But I have seen no discouragement. I bate not
one jot of hope. I believe that God rules above,
and that he will rule in the hearts of men, and
that, either with our aid or against it, he has determined to let the people go. But the confidence I have in my own mind that *the appointed
hour has nearly come* makes me feel all the more

confidence in the certain and final triumph of
our Union arms, because I do not believe that
this great investment of Providence is to be
wasted.'"

Governor Andrew was inaugurated Jan.
5, 1861. His final term as Governor ex-
pired Jan. 5, 1866. On that day he delivered to the two branches of the Legislature
a valedictory address. Without asserting,
with one of his biographers, that on this
address, "more than on any other production of his pen, rests his claim to the fame
of a great statesman," it must be admitted
by all that it was worthy of the man and
of the occasion. In logical acumen, in
clearness of statement, in breadth of view,
it is as remarkable as for moderation and
firmness. He was able to rise above the
plane of party spirit, above his own early
and intense feelings on the subject of
slavery, and to advocate doctrines as novel
to his own friends as they were surprising
to his enemies. The time has not yet come
when this production can be fairly judged

of, but there are few who will not recognize the wise and tolerant spirit of his utterance when he said: —

"I am satisfied that the mass of thinking men at the South accept the present condition of things in good faith ; and I am also satisfied that, with the support of a firm policy from the President and Congress, in aid of the efforts of their good faith, and with the help of a conciliatory and generous disposition on the part of the North, — especially on the part of those States most identified with the plan of emancipation, — the measures needed for permanent and universal welfare can surely be obtained.   There ought now to be *a vigorous prosecution of the peace*, just as vigorous as our recent prosecution of the war. We ought to extend our hands with cordial good-will to meet the proffered hands of the South ; demanding no attitude of humiliation from any ; inflicting no acts of humiliation upon any ; respecting the feelings of the conquered, notwithstanding the question of right and wrong between the parties belligerent. We ought, by all the means and instrumentalities of peace, and by all the thrifty methods of industry, by all the recreative agencies of education and religion, to help rebuild the waste places, and restore order, society, prosperity. Without industry and business there can be no progress. In their absence, civilized man even recedes towards barbarism. Let Massachusetts bear in mind the not unnatural suspicion which the past has engendered. I trust she is able, filled with emotions of boundless joy, and gratitude to Almighty God, who has given such victory and such honor to the right, to exercise faith in his goodness, without vain glory, and to exercise charity, without weakness, towards those who have held the attitude of her enemies."

The pecuniary means of Governor Andrew were always small. His practice had never been very lucrative, and his long public service effectually broke up the circle of his clients. On retiring from office, he determined to return to the bar, and declined various honorable and lucrative offices which were tendered to him. He soon entered upon a large practice, and was earning, at the time of his death, at the rate of thirty thousand dollars a year. One of the cases in which he was retained acquired such a prominence, and subjected

him to such reproaches as to require some
mention here. At the session of the General Court of Massachusetts, commencing
in January, 1867, petitions were presented
by upward of thirty thousand legal voters,
praying for the enactment of a judicious
license law, and for the regulation and control of the sale of spirituous and fermented
liquors in the Commonwealth. This petition was represented by Governor Andrew
and by the venerable Linus Child, who
called as witnesses a large number of respectable citizens from every profession
and occupation. The hearing occupied
more than a month and excited great interest, partly because it was the first time
the subject had received an examination
so thorough, but mainly from the fact that
there had never been so determined an
assault on the prohibitory law, on principle,
by men of marked character for ability and
high standing.

Governor Andrew summed up the case
in an elaborate argument and attacked the

doctrine of prohibitory legislation at the
root. It is, he argued, only in the strife
and controversy of life — natural, human,
and free — that robust virtue can be obtained, or positive good accomplished. It
is only in similar freedom, alike from
bondage and pupilage, alike from the pro-
hibitions of artificial legislation on the one
hand, and superstitious fears on the other,
that nations or peoples can become thrifty,
happy, and great.

In reply to the position that spirits and
wines are so alluring that health and morals
require teetotalism as the only safeguard;
that while there is evidence by which many
men, otherwise trustworthy, are convinced
in favor of a certain temperate dietetic use
by some people; yet, the moral dangers to
the mass are such that teetotalism ought not
only to be universally volunteered, but that
it ought to receive the vindication of the
statute-book and the moral support of the
Legislature, he said :—

"The whole argument involves one of the oldest of human errors ; so entirely human that it has no shadow of countenance from the religion of the New Testament. This world, in which while in the body we must abide, and this body, in which the spirit dwells, have been felt by many philosophers and moralists, both Christian and Heathen, to work a sad imprisonment of the celestial spirit. The immaculate purity of the spirit, soiled by any indulgence of the gross and material body, recedes from all human passion, and oftentimes from all intercourse with this tempting, dangerous, material world, to which alone in the temptation of a simple fruit, hanging on one of the trees of Eden, is due our whole experience of woe and the awful mystery of evil. The Church has always been tolerant, the Church of Rome has sometimes been too indulgent, of this mysticism ; while some of the Protestant sects, as well as of the societies in the Roman Church, have made it their vital principle. But it had its original expression in Oriental philosophy, not in Christianity, nor even in Judaism.

"When our Saviour came to the Jews, He found them mainly in these sects or divisions, — the Pharisees and the Sadducees. The latter, relatively small, maintained the law as written by Moses, denying the traditions of the Elders. They were rich, educated and influential, but

cold, hard and unspiritual. The Pharisees were
devoted to their religion, professed to live meanly,
to despise delicacies, to venerate the Elders.
But many of them, with ostentatious prayers,
sacrificed the heart of humanity on the altar of
ceremonious and hollow sanctity. Besides these,
were the Essenes. They were very few, and were
sincere, but narrow.

"Doubtless recruited from the sect of Pharisees they held rather to their general views,
which had an ascetic tendency. But, in a spirit
of devout, self-denying, mystic yearning after
God, they sought him in the ecstasies of contemplation, through exile, poverty and want;
instead of facing the world, bearing its social
burdens, risking its evils, temptations and woes."

.   .   .   .

"The Messiah accepted the recognition and
the baptism of John. But though He did this
honor to the prophet, and accepted his emblem
of the inward purifying of the soul, and of the
spiritual and celestial character of his own
coming, (as contrasted with some fierce appari-
tion of triumphant wrath,) the Saviour immediately made clear his own disagreement with the
dogmas of the Essenes, and the notions of asceticism.

"Soon after his baptism, there was a marriage-
feast. Invited to attend, He joined the festivity.

In compliance with the wishes of his Mother, the wine having failed, Jesus, by miracle, changed water into wine, and sent it to the master of the feast. 'Thus Jesus performed his first miracle at Cana, in Galilee, and *manifested his glory.*'[1] By these two actions, of emphatic significance,— that is, by attending the marriage-feast and making the wine,— our Lord, with the utmost publicity, placed himself in unequivocal antagonism to the asceticism of Nazarite and Essene, prevented his baptism from being mistaken for any profession of adhesion to the sect, the dogmas, or the practices of John; sanctioned the domestic tie, which the Essene contemned; the use of the beverage, which the Nazarite rejected; and the friendly enjoyment of innocent festivity.

"On no other theory can we understand the meaning of his joining the feast, or working the miracle. In the very hour of festivity the dreadful future of his Passion was presented to his soul. He sympathized with the social joy of others; but He was sad himself. Nor can we regard the miracle as wrought either to display his power, or simply for the hilarity of the feast. It would be to degrade the character of our Lord, and imagine motives to which He never yielded in the use of his heavenly gifts. If we perceive

---

[1] Gospel of St. John, ch. 2, v. 11. Norton's translation.

in his conduct the evident testimony He bore against opinions sincerely held by John, but of which He would not even *seem* to be the adherent, we shall better understand the spirit of the occasion, and the true character of our Lord, and we shall learn what Paul, the apostle, learned perhaps from the story of the same miracle (while Peter needed its revelation in vision), that ' *The kingdom of God is not meat and drink.*'

" Had Jesus been accessible to ordinary motives, He would have adopted, or at least indulged, asceticism. It would have given Him a party at the beginning of his career. It would have helped Him to defy, or to puzzle, the Pharisees, and to turn their weapons. But He was absorbed in the infinite purpose of a mission which included all human nature, all times, all places, and all circumstances of men."

This argument subjected him to great abuse and even vilification ; but nothing he ever did afforded him greater satisfaction than his action in this matter. The State election, a week after his death, completely revolutionized the policy of the Commonwealth and vindicated his position, although it could not protect him from the slanderous attacks of malignant philanthropy, for a course which he conscientiously adopted, and which was sustained and approved by many of the ablest and best men in the community.

Mr. Andrew died suddenly, on the 30th of October, 1867, of apoplexy. On the previous day he had been engaged in court. After tea some gentlemen called for a legal consultation. He suddenly complained of want of air in the room and endeavored to open a window. He staggered and was helped to the sofa, when he made earnest efforts to speak. A pencil was handed to him, which he vainly tried to use. He lingered in unconsciousness till the next evening at half-past six, when he died in the arms of his only brother, Isaac, who was in the act of raising him in bed to assist his breathing. The body was laid in Mount Auburn, but was subsequently removed to the old burial-place in Hingham, where a fine statue has been erected over his grave.

The death of Governor Andrew produced a great sensation throughout the country, and was suitably noticed by numerous public meetings. The bar meeting in Boston was presided over by Henry W. Paine, and was addressed by Richard H. Dana, Jr., George S. Hillard and others.[1]

So many writers and speakers have undertaken to delineate his character that nothing new remains to be said. Mr. Parke Godwin, at a meeting in the city of New York, happily summed it up in these few words: "Simple as a child in his manners; gentle as a woman in his affections; earnest as the enthusiast in his

---

[1] The writer of this sketch has made free use in it of his own remarks on that occasion. In 1865, a committee was appointed to procure a statue of Edward Everett, and five hundred subscribers contributed to this fund $33,000. After procuring a statue and a full-length portrait, a large sum remained. Of this, $10,000 were appropriated for a statue of John A. Andrew, in marble, to be placed in the State House. Thomas Ball was selected as the artist, and the statue was unveiled Feb. 14, 1871.

persuasions of truth; and steadfast as the martyr to his own interior faith; he was yet prudent, moderate, and wise, as the statesman, in his action." And Mr. William M. Evarts well expressed the feelings of those who knew the Governor most intimately: "We do not err at all when we say and feel that, up to the time of his death, to human observation, he had been preparing himself and gaining that opinion of mankind, that fame which after death is superior to power in life, which was to enable him to fill a greater, a wider, and a more useful part in the future of our country."

Of this remarkable man it may be truly said, that he was fortunate in the circumstances of his life and in those of his death. The son of parents of very different but extraordinary traits, his early training was under influences of the best kind, while there was never a jar in this happy family, which was a fair representative of the best in New England.

There was no lavish expenditure in the education of the oldest son ; but he had every advantage that he desired, was always fairly well supplied with money, and never had to endure the mortifications and trials of those who are obliged to obtain the means for their own education. His disposition was so fine, his spirits so equal, his temperament so hopeful, and his general health so good, that the carking cares and petty trials and vexations which impede the course or make wretched the early life of many men, were never his portion. All this should be a consolation to those who study his history and regret their own deficiencies when compared with such an example. Governor Andrew was fortunate in living at a time when his peculiar talents could be used to such vast advantage in public affairs. It is a cheap and not uncommon criticism of successful public men, that at other times and under other circumstances they would have made no mark. But "there's a divinity that shapes our ends." In great emergencies the man finally appears who is fitted to take the lead, and, under Providence, conduct affairs to a successful result. To say that any remarkable character is fitted for a particular epoch is merely to admit, what all religious men believe, that there is a guiding Hand above and beyond all human transactions. There has also been much unprofitable discussion as to what constitutes a great man, and whether true greatness and goodness can be distinct. The dispute is a matter of definitions. But all must agree that a successful man in the ordinary meaning of the term may be neither great nor good.

Governor Andrew was successful beyond ·the lot of most men in the worldly understanding of the term, and he was at the same time a good man in the best and highest sense. And his great success was in kind and degree such as would not have been predicted until it came. He was not an orator, when judged by the highest

standards, for he lacked the early culture
which is essential to one who aspires to
the noble distinction implied by that term.
But he was an impressive and persuasive
speaker of considerable power.   He was
not a polished writer, from the same defect;
for his rhetoric was often faulty, and he had
never had the highest training in this regard.   But there was a charm about some
of his productions that few men of culture
could fail to appreciate.   Nor was he a
statesman in the sense that Chatham and
Burke and Bolingbroke were statesmen.
Nor a great lawyer in the sense that Webster and Pinkney and Marshall were great
lawyers.   He died at the age of Webster
when he made the speech against Hayne
in the Senate of the United States.   It is
more than probable that if Governor Andrew had lived he would have taken rank
among the highest in the profession.

And yet this man was a great instrumen-
tality in the most important and grandest
controversy that is recorded in history.

With the civil war his name will always be identified. As the great " War Governor " he will always be known. In what then did his greatness consist? The answer is and always must be, " In his *character.*" He was most emphatically what Milton calls *a square and constant mind.* He stands to-day the embodiment and representative of manliness, simplicity, truthfulness, justice, — of all the qualities which go to make up the spiritual substance of our being, which is all we can take with us when we leave this world, and which will never cease to influence those who may occupy the places we now occupy, and who may try to do the works that are set before us to do.

Mr. Andrew was married Christmas evening, December, 1848, to Miss Eliza Jane, daughter of Charles Hersey, of Hingham. They had four children living at the time of his death, — John Forrester, born Nov. 26, 1850; Elizabeth Loring, born July 29,

1852; Edith, born April 5, 1854; Henry Hersey, born April 28, 1858. The family still occupy the home in Charles Street, Boston, where he died.

PERSONAL REMINISCENCES.

THE request to write some personal reminiscences. of Governor Andrew has been acceded to with considerable hesitation. Whoever undertakes a labor of this sort subjects himself to the imputation of giving importance to trifles of no public interest. But such things, when they aid in reproducing a life-like image of a noble and distinguished character, are worth recording. In this hope the following has been prepared.

PERSONAL REMINISCENCES.

My acquaintance with Governor Andrew
commenced at college, where we were not
at all intimate, as I preceded him by three
years. When I had nearly completed my
novitiate at No. 4 Court Street, in Boston, Andrew, who had recently graduated
(1837), made his appearance at the office
of Hubbard & Watts, where an old school-
mate and life-long friend, Cyrus Woodman,
was studying law, and asked if he knew
any lawyer who would take him as a student. Mr. Woodman thought of Henry
H. Fuller, the senior member of the firm
of Fuller & Washburn, and going at once
to their office on the northerly side of State
Street, opposite the Old State House, introduced his friend to Mr. Fuller. After

some pleasant talk Mr. Fuller kindly consented to receive him, and there he began his law studies a few weeks later, in the early days of November. The affectionate intimacy of these two men, so utterly different in tastes, appearance and character, was one of the things to be seen in order to be appreciated.

I was then living at the excellent boarding-house of Mrs. Ann Blodgett, in Howard Street (now a small hotel called the Woodbine), and Andrew came there to reside. We occupied adjoining rooms; neither of us aspired to first-class accommodations in the house, such as the decently paid clerks in shops could afford, and especially the gallant militia colonel, who sat at the head of the table and occupied the best room. We enjoyed the attic story. My own room was no room at all, but a mere closet, with just space enough for a small bed (I think there was a bureau; there certainly was a wash-stand) and a chair. It had no window whatever, but an opening into the entry that served for air and such light as could get in by way of the sky-light. It was called the "Captain's Office," from a supposed resemblance to that apartment on steamboats.

Our mutual friend, Mr. Woodman, who early left what his friends deemed the certain prospect of honorable success in Boston, for a prosperous business life in the West, occupied the larger room of the same attic, lighted by a window in the roof, which could be raised at one end. He gladly offered to share this apartment with his friend, who as gladly accepted the offer. The expense to each was thereby lessened, not an unimportant consideration at that time. On the whole, I preferred the windowless room at the same cost, with single blessedness.

We three were favorites of the landlady, and always fared well at the table. She was doubtless conscious that the rooms we occupied were not in great demand, and so desired us to remain. Taking a mate myself at the respectable age of twenty-one, I left the attic and the house; but Andrew remained there several years, and my closet was soon taken by a young student who has since made himself a leading member of the profession.[1]

On his admission to the bar, Mr. Andrew took an office at No. 19 Court Street, occupying the same room with Mr. N. T. Dow, an able but somewhat eccentric lawyer, who was afterwards associated with Mayor Prince, and is now deceased.

---

[1] Mr. Benjamin H. Currier, for a long time assistant clerk of the Supreme Judicial Court, and now, at the age of more than fourscore years, an active practitioner at the bar, had a room in this attic. He got into the habit of singing the old psalm tunes in concert with Andrew. As they occupied different rooms and both had good lungs, their efforts were not conducive to sleep by those inmates of the house who enjoyed a morning nap, and who got more of Coronation, St. Martyn's, Dundee, China, and so forth, than they bargained for. Our landlady kept her boarders well in hand, and remonstrated one morning at the breakfast-table with Currier, who was the older of the two offenders, in a decided manner. But he stood by his guns, and closed the animated debate by an emphatic declaration, " I *will* sing praises_to my God in the morning as long as I live ! "

But on the first of October, 1842, he became associated with Mr. Fuller as partner, on the invitation of the latter, and so continued until he removed to No. 4 Court Street in 1846, where he occupied a room with Mr. T. P. Chandler until his election as governor.

His progress at the bar was slow: his youthful appearance and apparent indifference to success were not in his favor. But whatever business was intrusted to his hands was faithfully done ; and he early manifested great interest in the poor who had legal rights or remedies to be cared for, and especially in those who were charged with crime. No one who had a "hard case," with no money to pay for legal assistance, was ever turned away from his office for that reason ; and no one however guilty was denied whatever assistance his case was fairly entitled to receive.

A disposition and a reputation of this sort will bring clients enough, such as they are. Nor can any one outside of the profession justly appreciate how much good may be done by listening to the stories of the poor who are charged with crime, and by carefully investigating the circumstances of cases which to a casual observer have nothing but evil about them. "I thank God," a lawyer once exclaimed to Andrew, "that there is one man at the bar to look out for the poor devils of criminals who are guilty enough and have no friends and no money."

At the same time, such a reputation as that of Andrew had its inconveniences, not only for himself but for his neighbors. After he removed to No. 4 Court Street, the entry seemed occasionally to be full of miserable-looking wretches who were waiting for admission to his room. It made no difference to him. He bore the comments of other lawyers on his ragged crowd with entire equanimity. He did not defend the crime, or take the criminal to his heart; but he was always determined that a poor man convicted of an offence should have no greater punishment than he really deserved; and that he should not be condemned for want of assistance to bring out every thing in his favor that could be proved.

There is a remarkable instance, among others, of his voluntary interposition, where a man was convicted in Boston of piracy. Andrew had never spoken to him in his life; he was not of counsel at the trial, nor did he know any person related to the prisoner in any way. But he quietly devoted some weeks to preparation; went to Washington at his own expense without fee or reward or the hope of any, and pressed upon the attorney-general and the President (Buchanan) those considerations which he deemed proper to be considered in support of the application for executive clemency. The man's life was saved.

He was employed a good deal in divorce cases, especially on behalf of the weaker sex. One of his sympathetic temperament would be easily as well as deeply affected

by the circumstances ordinarily attending
such a business. An injured woman —
especially if she were poor, and more especially if she were interesting in manner —
would secure his most earnest efforts at
once. It must be confessed that in these
cases he was sometimes grossly deceived
by the fair sex, and the guilt which was as
plain as possible to others had no existence
in his opinion. Nor could he always re-
press his indignation that others did not
agree with him.

In a somewhat notorious case of this
sort, it was my fortune to represent the
injured husband where my friend was
counsel for the wife. After the trial had
proceeded a day or two, my associate and
I desired to avoid the scandalous publicity
of a further hearing; and as there was con-
clusive evidence of the woman's guilt, we
sent him word, and offered to make an
arrangement by which that fact need not
come out. He regarded this as a sort of
bluff, and was in the highest degree indig-

nant, sending back defiance in strong language, in which there were some pretty robust expressions that he would not have used in a Sunday-school address. " Tell your master," he shouted in conclusion to the astonished messenger, " I am not afraid of him and all his crew." After a long trial the decision was against him, but I doubt if he was ever convinced of its justice.

He gradually came into a different practice, where he was employed by rich clients in the management of important interests both civil and criminal. He "got up" his cases with great care and patience, made elaborate preparation, and displayed an ability and pertinacity which must have secured him a high position in the profession. Indeed, at the time of his death he was doing a lucrative and successful business.

Owing to a lack of early habits of application, it was difficult for him to sit down to hard work; and it was amusing to see him with his coat off in the midst of a pile of books digging out the legal roots with the painstaking effort of one to whom such study was not congenial, all the while telling stories and indulging in jocose remarks. But he had a manly courage, united to great pertinacity of purpose, and never left a point until he had thoroughly mastered it, although it cost him far more labor than it does those whose minds are early disciplined by earnest application to the prescribed studies of school and college.

So certain it is, that young men who waste their early years in idle pursuits must pay a penalty in the future, if their ambition is roused and they attempt to accomplish any grand purpose or desire success of a permanent kind. Andrew took low rank in his class at college. He was not in a certain sense idle, for he was a great reader; but he never applied himself like a man who "meant business" to the studies set before him, and he felt the neglect in all his after life.

It is worthy of remark, that, as his business increased, he was retained in some important cases involving grave questions of constitutional law. The untiring efforts he made, and the careful investigations which these cases required, trained and fitted his mind for the trying emergencies in which he was afterwards placed, so that he showed an aptitude and a familiarity with certain subjects, which the ordinary practitioner does not usually possess. He defended the parties indicted at Boston for rescuing the fugitive slave, Burns; he defended the British consul on a charge of violating the neutrality laws during the Crimean war; he argued the petition for a writ of *habeas corpus* to test the legality of the imprisonment of the Free-state officers of Kansas at Topeka. He was largely concerned in the preparation of a defence of John Brown in Virginia. These and other important cases (among them a defence of the slave yacht " Wanderer," against forfeiture), involving principles of international and interstate law, received careful examination at his hands, and brought forth fruit an hundred-fold in subsequent years.

In politics, he was an ardent and even an enthusiastic member of the Whig party from the start. On this point, his master in the law, Mr. Fuller, doubtless exercised some influence over him. He believed in the traditions, the principles and the policy of this great party; and he believed that by and through it the grand reforms he hoped to see would be ultimately accomplished.

He was also an anti-slavery man, an advocate of all measures that could be constitutionally adopted in relation to slavery. He was a warm personal friend of Mr. Garrison, but did not approve his methods, and was shocked by his asperities and indiscriminate denunciation of slaveholders; for he thought it was possible to hate slavery without hating every slaveholder, and to abolish it without destroying the Union. In a letter to Mr. Garrison, as late as 1860, he declared that he had often been pained at the unremitting and frequently unjust assaults by abolitionists on men whom he greatly respected, and whose services in the cause of national and impartial liberty he highly prized. "My fidelity," he added, "to the existing institution of government, its charters, its organization, and the duties of its citizenship, is, ever has been, and, I doubt not, will always be unshaken."

After the nomination of Fremont in 1856, he came to me and expressed much regret at the threatened disruption of the Whig party in Massachusetts. He declared that if the approaching Whig convention in Massachusetts would put a good ticket in the field, and take no action against the election of Fremont for president, he and his political friends would sustain the nominations and so strive to keep the grand old party alive in the Commonwealth. An effort was made in this direction, but some of the prominent leaders were so opposed to the course that nothing could be effected. Resolutions were reported by George S. Hillard, advocated by J. Thomas Stevenson, and adopted, signifying a preference for the candidate already nominated by the meanest political party (Native American) ever known in this country.   This course was intended as a declaration of war against Andrew and all who acted with him.   The record of that convention is a singular and interesting one to read now, in view of the cataclysm that came so soon.

The Whig party of Massachusetts went down with colors flying, and the political waters closed over the gallant ship and most who were on board.   Many of those who had remained with the organization up to this time were disheartened at the course pursued, and their chagrin was intensified by the fact, that the accomplished scholar and eminent statesman who presided at the convention set his face like flint against any compromise.   They complained that it was only necessary for the Whig party to carry out its own resolutions, adopted time and again in conventions and in the General Court, to save its organization and power in Massachusetts. They were charmed with the eloquence that portrayed the glories of the Constitution. They agreed to all the praises that were lavished on its Great Defender. They admired the courage that would assault the anti-slavery hosts which were gathering with an apparently irresistible force. But they felt — some of them — like the French General Bosquet, who said of the charge of the Light Brigade at Balaklava, "It was magnificent, but it was not war!"

As a political manager, Mr. Andrew was not a success. He was personally popular all his life and with all sorts of people; but when it came to matters of principle he was too straightforward, square and emphatic, to suit those who would like to accommodate their principles to special emergencies. Moreover, he was the most obstinate of men when he took a position, and singularly destitute, in a ward caucus, of that tact which is at once effective with the promiscuous crowd and those who are clothed in purple and fine linen. It is amusing and eminently suggestive to look back on those days of small things, when Sumner and Andrew and others like them would try in vain to accomplish something at the primary meetings.

There was at one time great excitement about the Boston schools, when Horace Mann had his controversy with the school committee. At No. 4 Court Street, we wished to have Charles Sumner chosen a member of the committee in old ward four, where he resided. Anticipating the difficulty of obtaining the nomination of one who had so little popularity with the people, and who uttered such pronounced opinions in regard to Mr. Mann, considerable preparation was made for the contest. Andrew lived in that ward and was relied on to manage the affair. It was a wretched failure, and the candidate who afterwards became so distinguished was severely snubbed by his own neighbors. Sumner was present, and I think not much surprised; although, as an intimate friend of Mr. Mann, he earnestly desired the place. But the indignation of John A. Andrew was great. In giving an account of the meeting, he wound up with this remark, in order to contrast Sumner's magnanimity with that of one of his opponents, " There was —— " (a disagreeable Cambridge graduate, who had an office in the street and affected to despise Sumner, and who has long since passed out of sight and memory), " he did all he could against Sumner, and the latter voted for *him* as one of the ward inspectors ! "

Mr. Andrew never seemed to have any ambition for public office. I hardly know by what influences he was induced to go to the lower house of the Legislature for 1858. But there could not have been a more propitious time for the exhibition of his peculiar talents, and for a popular application of his political principles. The great question of the session was the removal of Edward G. Loring from the office of Judge of Probate, which, it was alleged, he held in violation of a statute of the Commonwealth, rendering it incompatible with the office of United States commissioner. Mr. Loring in that capacity had ordered the surrender of the fugitive slave Burns.

By an act of the Legislature of 1855, it was declared that certain offices under the government of the United States are incompatible with offices of honor, emolument and trust in this Commonwealth. Acting on this provision, the General Court had several times by address requested in vain the removal of Judge Loring from office. When the subject came up again in 1858, Mr. Andrew entered upon the discussion with characteristic zeal and enthusiasm. On the other side was Caleb Cushing, one of the ablest parliamentarians our country has produced; a man thoroughly versed also in the principles of international law, of great logical acumen, of immense erudition,—cool, calm, inflexible in purpose and of a most persuasive eloquence. In learning, legislative experience, thorough scholarly discipline, and a familiar knowledge of all distinguished writers on international and constitutional law, there was no equality between the two combatants. But on this particular subject of slavery and the relations of the States as affected by that institution, the young legislator was a match for the older one; and he was so thoroughly in earnest and so in accord with the prevailing sentiments of a majority of the people, that he won a comparatively easy victory and became at a bound the acknowledged leader of the House. Few men ever made a great reputation so suddenly and held it during life.

Governor Banks, on presentation of the address, ordered Mr. Loring's removal. After the message was read, Mr. Cushing denounced the act in severe terms, declaring that Judge Loring was the first judicial officer in this country to be a victim to the execution of his sworn duty to the Constitution, according to his conscientious convictions, and prognosticated that the next blow would be struck at the judicial and constitutional independence of the Supreme Court of the United States. This brought Andrew to his feet, who made a short speech which was received with the greatest enthusiasm.

At the close of the session, he was offered a seat on the bench of the Supreme Judicial Court, which he declined, and he also refused to permit his name to be submitted to the convention of his party as a candidate for the nomination of Governor. "But in 1860, notwithstanding this abstinence from official life, he was nominated for Governor by a genuine popular impulse which overwhelmed the old political managers, who regarded him as an intruder upon the arena, and had laid other plans."

My personal intimacy with him did not

cease on his elevation to the chair of state. For some time we had not been in accord on political matters, so far as they were affected by the anti-slavery agitation. We had a good many discussions and some warm ones on these and kindred topics; but they never affected our personal relations. When the war was actually begun, all minor differences disappeared, and the whole community was soon united in one purpose to preserve the Union. I was in the Legislature the second and third years after he was inaugurated as Governor; and my personal observation justifies the statement of Colonel Browne, that, in his conduct as Governor, Mr. Andrew's "independence of partisan control alienated from him all the trading politicians, and would have broken down an ordinary man in caucuses and conventions, but he possessed a strength which was independent of small political managers. They were always against him; and the influence of almost all the old leaders of his party was against him, also, from

the day he was first named as Governor."[1]
So strong was this influence in the Legislature, that it was at one time almost fatal
to any measure if it were known that he
desired it, and occasionally the aid of a
well-known war Democrat was relied on to
introduce or advocate bills, so that it might
not be supposed that the executive took
any especial interest in them.

This is a convenient place for the remark, that the Governor was fortunate in
securing the services as military secretary
of his intimate friend, Albert G. Browne,
Jun., Esq., a gentleman of first-class ability,
highly educated, a good lawyer, and a radical abolitionist. Colonel Browne had
wonderful powers of endurance: he never
seemed to be fatigued, or worried, or anxious. He understood the Governor better
than any other man living, and they *worked
in together* famously; so harmoniously, in
fact, that to see them on opposite sides of

[1] Browne's Sketch of the Military Life of Governor
Andrew.

the table in the Governor's room, one might sometimes be almost in doubt which was the chief executive officer of the Commonwealth.

The value of Colonel Browne's services in those trying times was inestimable, and they were fully appreciated by his distinguished friend, although he himself never paraded them before the public, or appeared to regard them as anything remarkable. He was subsequently appointed by Governor Bullock reporter of the decisions of the Supreme Judicial Court, and held the office several years. It should be added that the Sketch of Governor Andrew by his military secretary is the best account of him that exists. Nothing can be more accurate and life-like than the following:—

"The arrangement of the private executive rooms at the State House was unchanged during the whole of the Governor's administration. It was faulty in many respects, and a few simple changes in it, enabling him to seclude himself, would have saved him from much care and annoyance. They were on the same floor with the

Council Chamber, and were reached through a long and narrow corridor which led into an antechamber. Out of this the Governor's apartment opened directly, with no intervening room. It was a low-studded chamber, perhaps twenty-five feet square, lighted by two windows opening westward. In the centre was a massive square table, on the side of which, facing the door of the antechamber, the Governor had his seat. Directly opposite him, at the same table, sat his secretary. At a desk near one of the windows was the place of an assistant secretary. The chairs and sofa were very plain and covered with green plush. The large bookcases along the northern wall, empty at the beginning of his administration, became filled before the end of it with more than two hundred volumes of the correspondence conducted under his immediate direction. A large mirror, with a heavily carved black-walnut frame surmounted the mantel, gas-fixtures projecting from among the carving ; and on these during the first year of the war, while Massachusetts was arming and equipping her own troops, he was accustomed to hang specimens of shoddy clothing or defective accoutrements, labelled with the names of the faithless contractors, thus publicly exposed to the indignation of the hundreds of visitors who frequented the room. His only means of seclusion was to retreat into a room beyond the antechamber, from which there was no other outlet than the door of entrance, which was of solid iron. Every frequenter of the State House may remember seeing him, after being pestered beyond endurance, hasten across the antechamber into this room, where he would bolt and bar out the waiting crowd until he could finish some urgent work demanding freedom from the interruptions to which he was subject in his own apartment. Once behind that iron door, he was free ; and it was the only place in the whole building where he was secure from intrusion.

" His patience, however, under all manner of interruption was marvellous. Now and then it would give way in little acts of nervousness, such as pulling unconsciously at a bell-rope which hung over his table, or insisting on the immediate attendance of an old and favorite clerk from the Adjutant-General's office who had been dead a year or more. By some curious psychological process, when the Governor had been especially vexed at anything which went wrong in that office, he more than once forgot the old gentleman's death, and sent down stairs for him."

" In those five years of his administration," says the military secretary, " he tasted the cares and sorrows, the hopes and joys, and concentrated the labors of a century of ordinary life ; and such an experience aggravated his tendency to the disease which at last was fatal.   No soldier struck by a rebel bullet on the battle-field died more truly a victim to the national cause."

It was touching to see how often the Governor vainly sought some actual seclusion and rest from engrossing cares. He was tried almost beyond endurance when suffering from the severe headaches to which he was constitutionally subject. Of a Sunday morning, he would come down to my house, take his breakfast of the Yankee dish of baked beans and brown bread, and late in the forenoon make his way " across lots " over the unfrequented streets of the Back Bay in season to hear the sermon of James Freeman Clarke. But on working-days there seemed no respite.   If he remained at the State House, there could of course be no real seclusion.   If he went to his own home, the door would be besieged by an importunate crowd. If he took a room at a hotel, the fact would soon be known, and there could be no peace after that. On one occasion, when greatly suffering from headache, he sought the house of a friend where he was very intimate. There was no one at home, the servant said. Well, then, he would go upstairs and lie down. When the lady of the mansion came in from her morning calls, she was greatly astonished and somewhat amused to find the Governor of the Commonwealth fast asleep on her bed.

Colonel Browne remarks that the Governor "in his military appointments never asked what were the political associations of the candidates, provided only they were loyal men. General Butler, whom he designated to the command of the Massachusetts militia sent to rescue Washington in 1861, had been the candidate of the Breckenridge party for Governor, in opposition to himself."

"*Provided only they were loyal men.*"   It was on this ground that he rejected the services of Caleb Cushing.   He had private information, which he considered reliable, of Cushing's stimulating Virginia into secession in the spring of 1861 during a visit to Richmond, and entertained a general distrust of his loyalty.   But this distinguished citizen was soon afterwards employed by the State Department at Washington; and he went to South Carolina, just before the firing on Fort Sumter, on a confidential mission at the suggestion of judges of the Supreme Court of the United States.

On his tender of services, the Governor acted with great promptitude.   The correspondence on this subject is preserved in the archives of the Commonwealth.

Newburyport, April 25, 1861.

Sir, — I beg leave to tender myself to you, in any capacity, however humble, in which it may be possible for me to contribute to the public weal in the present critical emergency.

I have no desire to survive the overthrow of the government of the United States; I am ready for any sacrifice to avert such a catastrophe; and I ask only to be permitted to lay down my life in the service of the Commonwealth and of the Union.

I am, very respectfully,

C. CUSHING.

His Excellency JOHN A. ANDREW,
Governor of the Commonwealth.

———◆———

COMMONWEALTH OF MASSACHUSETTS,
EXECUTIVE DEPARTMENT,
BOSTON, April 27, 1861.

Hon. CALEB CUSHING,

SIR,— Under the responsibilities of this hour, — remitted both as a man and a magistrate to the solemn judgment of conscience and honor,— I must remember only that great cause of constitutional liberty and of civilization itself referred to the dread arbitrament of arms. And I am bound to say that although our personal relations have always been agreeable to myself, and notwithstanding your many great qualities fitting you for usefulness; yet your relation to public affairs, your frequently avowed opinions touching the ideas and sentiments of Massachusetts; your intimacy of social, political and sympathetic intercourse with the leading secessionists of the Rebel States, maintained for years, and never (unless at this moment) discontinued, — forbid my finding you any place in the council or the camp. I am compelled sadly to declare that, were I to accept your offer, I should dishearten numerous good and loyal men, and tend to demoralize our military service. How gladly I would have made another reply to your note of the 25th inst., which I had the honor to receive yesterday, I need not declare, nor attempt to express the painful reluctance with which this is written.

Faithfully your obedient servant,
JOHN A. ANDREW,
Governor.

Mr. Cushing's letter was accompanied by the following: —

[Unofficial.]
NEWBURYPORT, April 25, 1861.

DEAR SIR, — I pray you not to regard the accompanying proffer in any light other than that of earnest solicitude on my part to discharge my duty to our common country. Permit me to assume that in our past political relations, as certainly as in our personal ones, there has been nothing to forbid me to make, or you to receive, such a proffer at the present time.

You alone are able to judge whether in the scope of official duties, there is anything to assign to me to do. If there be, or not, I pray you to say so to me in all sincerity, in order that, having thus placed myself at your discretion, I may, if not needed directly by you, then decide according to my own judgment what to undertake.

I am, very respectfully,

C. CUSHING.

Governor ANDREW.

Mr. Cushing was a good deal touched by this affair, and spoke of it with more feeling than he usually exhibited in matters personal to himself. He told me he should make a formal reply to the Governor's letter, or place among his papers a statement which would be his justification in the future. That he did neither may be attributed, perhaps, to a consciousness that he had used strong expressions in regard to secession, or he may have been consoled by the confidence which was reposed in his present loyalty by eminent persons at Washington.

Governor Andrew more often made mistakes in regard to men than measures. This arose in part from his sympathetic nature: for, although no one who knew him could suppose for a moment that he would appoint a personal friend to a position for which he considered him incompetent or not the best fitted, he was sometimes so attracted by certain prominent characteristics as to overlook deficiencies; and, on the other hand, he was sometimes so shocked by glaring faults as to be unable to appreciate excellences which were obvious to others. His tendency was so strong to protect and even favor the oppressed or those who were under a cloud, and even those who were criminal, that he would go far out of his way and strain a point to assist them. Some of his friends occasionally thought that he acted unreasonably in this regard.

There was the case of Green, who was convicted and sentenced to be hung for one of the most cool, dastardly, and cruel murders for money ever recorded in the annals of crime. The Governor was opposed to capital punishment, but understood the proprieties of his position too well to nullify the existing law. He ordered the execution of Desmarteau in 1861, of Hersey in 1862, and of Callender in 1863. But he made up his mind that Green was not properly tried, and he never changed that opinion. It was extraordinary to see with what pertinacity he followed the matter. He refused to sign the warrant for execution during his term of office, and there most men would have left the case. Not so with him. He pursued his successor for a commutation of sentence, and appeared before the executive council. He prepared a legal argument for the court and did all he could to influence the press. I always supposed that his personal interviews with the convict in prison operated very strongly. He was full of the subject and would talk about it for hours. "Everybody," he once exclaimed, "who has seen

Green knows that he is not fit to be hung!" This was perhaps the real point. He regarded the culprit as a weak, feeble, half-witted boy, not a proper subject for the gallows.

A friend once told him that he had seen a man frequently coming out of the State House, whom they had both known and respected for years, but whose conduct the friend had been professionally called upon to investigate. The party had been criminally false in a trust and admitted it, although he had done what he could to make restitution, and professed great sorrow. The Governor flushed up as he heard the story, and exclaimed: "Well, I'll trust him. I am going to appoint him to an office." Reasons were given why he ought not to be trusted, but the more they were urged, the firmer the Governor was that the man should have another chance.

A young man was appointed to a somewhat confidential position in the State House, who had been pardoned out of prison by the President of the United States on Andrew's solicitation, in which he was aided by Edward Everett. The young convict was extremely useful, but kept up his crooked ways in a degree until a formal remonstrance was made to the Governor. The latter said if he turned him off he would go straight to destruction, and preferred the responsibility of his disreputable practices to his utter ruin. But the official's conduct became so bad at last that he was discharged.

It was of this person that a witty vagabond, whom the Governor always befriended, once said to a clerk in the State House: "John [the governor] is trying to make something of Blank, but he can't. I tell you that the man who is imprisoned for a long term for stealing and gets pardoned out, and when he goes away *steals the jail syringe*, has got it in him to steal!" It should be said of the author of this remark that he never did anything worse than get drunk, but he was very bad indeed in this respect, and was once imprisoned for the offence in the same jail with the young man above referred to. Subsequently when he was at the Washingtonian Home, the Governor sent him some money by " Blank." But he refused to take it, and wrote to the Governor requesting him to send it by some one else, as he was *trying to reform, and proposed to cut all his state-prison acquaintances.*

- It should be stated here, that while the Governor was disposed to overlook a person's bad antecedents in the hope of a reform, and always desired to " give him another chance," he could not be persuaded to do a public injustice, by the appointment of men to positions for which they were not in his judgment competent. He had firmness enough when occasion called for it.

When a certain officer desired promotion, and great efforts were made by his friends in his behalf, the Governor was satisfied that he was not the man for the place:

he had made careful inquiries. Many citizens came to the State House to ask for the commission: "The Irish would enlist under this man." It was of no use. Later, a large delegation of leading men came in a body, resolved to get the commission. They labored with the Governor two hours. He was courteous, but firm. They withdrew into an anteroom for consultation, and soon after returned with this suggestion: "If we go home and come to-morrow and bring old Governor Lincoln with us, and he will indorse this man, will you commission him?" The Governor rose up, and bringing his fist down on the table, said: "Gentlemen, if he was as good a soldier as Julius Cæsar, and you should bring an angel from heaven to indorse him, knowing what I do, I would not commission him!"

The same remark as to the Governor's partial or imperfect judgment of men may be applied in a larger way to his course in regard to the nomination of President

Lincoln the second time. He was very active in the movement in 1864 to displace the President. The secrecy with which this branch of the Republican politics of that year has been ever since enveloped .is something marvellous; there were so many concerned in it. When it *all* comes out, if it ever does, it will make a curious page in the history of the time. The signal for the abandonment of the movement was first made in a speech by Mr. Chase, in accordance with the general opinion of the "conspirators," that it was inexpedient to press it further after the Democratic proceedings at Chicago. Governor Andrew lived long enough to see the error of all this. Indeed, after the re-nomination of Lincoln he was engaged to speak in behalf of his re-election to mass meetings in many of the principal towns in New York.

This is no place for a discussion of the reasons for the anti-Lincoln movement; but it is only just to say, that the reports from Washington in 1863 did impute a frivolity of language and demeanor in the President, which could not but offend many earnest men, and were artfully used by eminent persons in Washington to create dissatisfaction. There was a characteristic anecdote related, which had no especial tendency to render the President popular at the State House in Boston.

The Legislature had been famous for passing resolutions against slavery. After the war began, the patriotic spirit of members soon showed itself in the same tendency. But there were some who thought the time for this sort of thing had passed, and everything offered was referred to a committee who brought in a resolve in the fewest words possible. A friend of the Governor, who also held an official position, desired to present it personally to the President. It was accordingly written on parchment, with the great seal annexed, and plenty of red tape. Arrived in Washington, the messenger by appointment met the President at eleven o'clock the next day, to present this resolve of the Commonwealth of Massachusetts. The Chief Magistrate of the nation sat in an armchair, with one leg over the elbow, while the emissary of Massachusetts presented the parchment with a little speech. The President took the document, slowly unrolled it, and remarked in a quaint way, " Well, it is n't long enough to scare a fellow"! It is not remarkable that the Massachusetts official said as he left the room, " That is certainly an extraordinary person to be President of the United States!"

After Governor Andrew had renewed his practice at the bar, he was retained as counsel for upwards of thirty thousand petitioners for the enactment of a judicious license law. In his famous argument before the committee, he only expressed the honest convictions he had entertained for years. He used wine himself, and most heartily despised the prevailing hypocrisy as to its use by others. As Governor, he would have brought the subject of a license law before the Legislature, and urged some practical legislation in opposition to the principle of absolute prohibition, but for a fear that it might be the occasion of divided counsels in regard to the great and absorbing subject of the war. He did not hesitate to utter his views with entire distinctness in private, and nothing gave him greater satisfaction than his efforts before the committee of the Legislature, where he appeared as counsel.

He knew that this course would subject him to reproach; but probably he never did suppose men would go to the length of charging him with being himself an intemperate person, — as foul a slander as was ever uttered about a public character. He knew too well, from his intercourse with the poor and the unfortunate, the enormous evils of intemperance, to advocate any legislation which he supposed would tend to its increase; and in his own case he had that absolute self-control which rendered him safe from this and similar temptations.   He had profound respect for all who abstained absolutely from the use of wine, either on their own account or for example to others; but he demanded equal respect for his own discretion, and no personal considerations could restrain him from a full and free expression of his opinions.

The first time he ever spoke in public was at the age of fourteen, and on the subject of temperance.   The circumstances were peculiar, and are well described by his brother Isaac in a letter to a friend. It is worth copying here: —

" It has often been alluded to in print, but the particulars have never been correctly given ; at least in no account that I have ever seen.   Believing that you will be glad to know the circumstances connected with that address, I will relate them.   When we resided in Windham, Maine, at our old birthplace, there was a temperance society organized.   Whether Albion's name was upon the roll or not I do not now remember.   Perhaps not, as he was at that time a mere boy.   The president of the society was a very worthy Free-will Baptist clergyman by the name of Shaw. One of the most prominent men in the society was Mr. Josiah Little, a neighbor of ours, and a nephew to Dr. Timothy Little, the celebrated surgeon of Portland at that time.

"Previous to holding one of their meetings, which was appointed for a Sabbath afternoon, the officers of the society and some others wanted to get my brother to make some remarks in the meeting. Though he was at this time, as I have already said, but a boy, and one whom they had all known from his birth, they had such confidence in his abilities that they felt satisfied he could speak to the purpose if called upon to try. Having obtained father's consent, Mr. Little spoke to Albion about it. Having learned that his father was willing, Albion readily agreed to accede to their wishes. It was a pleasant afternoon when the meeting was held, and there was a full attendance. The people were much interested in the temperance cause, and the house was well filled. The place of meeting was the Free Meeting House, as it was called. This house was not far from Horsebeef Falls on the Windham side of the river, and less than a mile from my father's. Albion took his seat with the audience near the rear of the house, and a little to the speaker's right. After the president of the society had delivered his address and some others had spoken upon the subject, Albion was called upon to make some remarks. I well remember the time, place and scene. Occupying a seat close behind him, I had a good chance to hear as well as watch him. He rose to his feet cool, calm and collected, with the dignity of a man and the modesty of a child, and began. Commencing with the child who is early taught to partake of alcoholic drinks, and following him along his downward career, he pictured his wretched end. In contrast to this was shown the onward and upward life of those who early resolved upon a life of temperance; and to illustrate this point he directed his hearers to look upon some eminent men whose names he gave them.

"The company was held almost spell-bound. Such an address from a mere child. Elder Shaw afterwards said to my father: 'Albion beat us all.' It *was* good. Had this speech come from some mature man, it would have been highly creditable to him: how much more to a boy of about fourteen years of age! Though forty years have passed away since that occurrence, I can distinctly see in my mind's eye that short, fat, chubby, curly-headed little fellow, as he stood in the old meeting-house, and with such earnestness and eloquence, gesticulating with his right arm, advocated the cause of temperance and besought the young as well as the old to beware of strong drink. That meeting-house is gone. The officers of the old temperance society have long since passed away. Worthy men they were, and worthy of being held in grateful remembrance ; and they as well as all who heard him, remembered with love and respect the youthful orator, who gave his first public address on that beautiful Sabbath afternoon.

"You, who knew him so well, know that the expectations in regard to him, raised so early, were not disappointed, except by his premature death."

Perhaps the two most notable things about Governor Andrew were his religious fervor and his mirthfulness. He was generally familiar with the Bible and studied portions of it very carefully. The hymns of Dr. Watts he seemed to know by heart. In the early days in Boston, nothing gave him greater satisfaction than the Bible instructions of James Freeman Clarke. He was especially interested in the epistles of Paul, and used frequently to enlarge, at my house, upon the teachings of his pastor at the vestry. His faith was deep and earnest, without a touch of cant, for he spoke on religious subjects with the same ease and freedom that he did on any others, and never indulged in a didactic strain.

One time late in the night, as we were returning in a carriage from a country caucus, where we had made speeches, a discussion arose on the subject of prayer. He spoke emphatically of the childlike simplicity of the early Christians in asking and expecting certain specific results from supplication to God. He alluded to the great comfort it was to him to *lay out the whole case*, in the full belief that it would be in some way effective. " I want," he said, " to tell the story in my own way, although I know it is impossible for me to give any information to the Almighty."

At the bar meeting after his death, George S. Hillard, a political opponent but life-long friend, declared that he " never knew a man whose daily life and conversation embodied the teachings of the Saviour as laid down in Holy Writ more than his.

He never knew a man who left this world with less of the stain of sin than he." Richard H. Dana at the same meeting said: " He could not be deflected from the course of duty by any of the temptations which address themselves to the weaknesses of public men. His morality was not a graft of later years upon an ordinary stock; it was not sweet water gathered into a vase, nor the accumulations of a large reservoir; but it was a fountain of living water, springing up from the depths of his nature. The foundations of his character were laid deep and strong."

His pastor, Mr. Clarke, has frequently given public testimony to the religious character of his parishioner and to the value of his services in the church. His heart was in this thing. He gave more time and devotion in this direction than will ever be known in this world; for many of his works were as quiet and unostentatious as they were earnest and effective. Numerous instances might be mentioned of the depth of his interest in a religious life. Here is one that has a touch of the romantic.

On the last day of the year, the Governor was once hard at work in the State House till near midnight. No one else but the messenger was in the building; without was a driving storm. The Governor suddenly dropped his pen, looked at his watch and said, " It is twenty-five minutes to twelve. Do you know that at this time, down at Father Taylor's church, they are praying out the year? Now if you can get a conveyance in time, you and I will go down and help them." They got down in time. Father Taylor clapped his hands, and gave other expressions of his gladness at the Governor's visit; and the speech which Andrew made to the audience huddled into that little church, from the description of a person who was present, was one of the most moving, pathetic and eloquent he ever made in his life.

Of his disposition, Colonel Browne truly says, it was more than cheerful: it was merry. He had many and severe trials, — much to weigh upon his spirits; but, even in the saddest moods and sometimes when in physical pain and suffering, a humorous remark or a good story affected him pleasantly at once, his countenance would lighten up, and he would seldom fail to do his share in repartee or kindred anecdote. There seemed to be no end to the stories he could tell. He enjoyed them himself and his loud ringing laugh was really inspiring.[1]

---

[1] One night at the theatre, many years ago, his laughter at the acting of Collins, the Irish comedian, was so uproarious as to attract general attention. The construction put by sombre critics on the famous line,

> "And the loud laugh that speaks the vacant mind,"

that loud laughter is a trait of *inane* or *empty* minds is exploded. *A mind free from care* is what the poet meant in the opinion of a great English humorist and sound critic; although it must be admitted that laughter and bright smiles and even humorous sallies may sometimes conceal a sadness which lies deep in the heart, a fact that has not escaped the attention of a minor poet : —

> "I often smile to hide the tear I shed;
> As when the jester's bosom swells,
> And mournfully he shakes his head,
> We hear the jingling of his bells."

He was a mimic of considerable power, and, having a retentive memory, could repeat whole passages from the arguments of lawyers or the sermons of ministers in the precise manner of the speakers. His occasional imitations of characters in the remote towns of Maine were very droll. It made no difference where he was or who was present, he would work himself into an excitement that startled those who were not familiar with his style in this regard.

In this matter he acted on principle, as well as in obedience to the impulses of his nature. He never omitted on suitable occasions an effort to inspire others with his own sunny and hopeful views of life and duty. Some of the main causes which combined to increase the perils of New-Englanders from drunkenness he declared, on a public occasion, to be a "hard climate, much exposure, few amusements, a sense of care and responsibility cultivated intensely, and the prevalence of ascetic and gloomy theories of life, duty and Providence."

Solemn citizens, who did not quite approve of such fun in the Governor of the Commonwealth, would look very grave. Sometimes their astonishment was the most amusing thing of all, reminding one of the declaration of a good man who was amazed at the development of unexpected traits in a neighbor: "We are fearfully and wonderfully mixed."[1]

It must not be inferred that he was frivolous or vulgar in this overflow of his exuberant spirits; still less, that he ever used his power to bring ridicule or contempt

[1] It must be confessed, too, that in the trials and embarrassments of those days, especially in regard to matters where there was inefficiency or neglect of duty, the Governor would occasionally give a place to vigorous expletives not found in the New England Primer. But the circumstances were always such, that it is safe to say these expressions formed no part of the Recording Angel's page. Indeed, they were entirely out of the Governor's line ; but, when resorted to, they were chosen and applied with the skill of a veteran, and were used with such fervor, and fitted so well, that, as Longfellow says of Miles Standish : —

"Sometimes it seemed a prayer, and sometimes it sounded
like swearing."

upon others. Although often ready to exclaim,

"Mirth, admit me of thy crew,"

no man was more mindful of the feelings of others, or a greater stickler for the proprieties of official position or for the respect due to sacred things. One who knew him well, in view of his many-sided character, declared that he was a delightful combination of Jupiter and Pickwick! The cloud-compelling Jove! — yes. But Pickwick? — The gentle cockney had no sense of humor!

It is stated elsewhere in this volume, that the home of Governor Andrew's father was the usual resort of ministers when visiting or journeying through the town. These men were not only the best educated people of the day in that region, but were, as a rule, remarkably cheerful. Generally settled for life and thus assured of their support, they had a cheerful bearing and a practical sense of humor which was often in remarkable contrast with the doctrines they taught in the pulpit: they held a position and had an influence which can scarcely be appreciated at this day.

Always welcome guests, tradition says it was good to see them — especially when there were several together — before the huge blazing fire in the best room of a farmer's house, where a mug of flip or a glass of something that had made a voyage from the West Indies, and cider *ad libitum*, were not at all out of the way, and perhaps contributed somewhat to the quiet mirth of the evening.[1]

From early association with men like these, Andrew got something of his humor, many of his clerical anecdotes, and a portion of his familiarity with the Bible and

[1] They were all politicians, free and outspoken, and generally in the time of the embargo and war, Federalists. On one occasion, when General Fessenden, father of the senator and a leader of the party, delivered a Fourth of July oration in New Gloucester, Parson Moseley read with an unction which showed whom he alluded to, the hymn commencing : —

> " Break out their teeth, Almighty God!
> Those teeth of lions dyed in blood ! "

the hymn-book; nor could one of his observing character fail to be interested in the earnest piety, sincere devotion to duty, and manly bearing of these servants of God.

His mirthfulness was increased by contact with the people. In no part of the world is there a keener sense of humor than among the rural population of Maine. Before the temperance reform, this was more marked than at the present time; owing to the fact, in part, that there are fewer occasions for its exercise. The country store is no longer a place where the people congregate of an evening and take a social glass. The village inns have almost disappeared; and the workmen do not now "knock off" at eleven o'clock in the forenoon and at four in the afternoon for a glass of grog and a pipe.

He must be a bold man who should express a wish for the return of those old times, with all the attendant evils of drunkenness, poverty and crime. The farmers of to-day are prosperous: some of them are rich. They toil and moil. They sow and reap and gather into barns, and are eminently respectable. But still the fact remains, that the rural population are by far less cheerful than they were in the days referred to. The love of fun is in them; and the young men, who find little on the farms to satisfy this affection, are discontented and seek the cities, where there are harmless amusements they cannot find at home, and a freedom denied them in the country towns. The farms are deserted by youth to an extent that is almost appalling, and the next generation will find many of them lying waste or occupied by a foreign population.

Whoever strives to correct this gloomy tendency of the people is building better than he knows, and doing more for society than those can appreciate who think the chief end of man is to "live like a hermit and work like a horse," in order to gain riches or fame or power, and transmit to posterity a name which is covered with the odor of respectability and nothing more.

Governor Andrew did his full share to counteract this tendency to gloom and despair. His daily life was a plea for cheerfulness. Always in sympathy with the misfortunes of others; always ready to assist the poor, the sick, and even the guilty, he had no respect for morbid sorrows, and no patience with doctrines that called for vengeance rather than pity for the wicked.

Mirthfulness is often a marked trait in large natures, and is a wonderful aid to those who are oppressed with care and anxiety, or whose daily avocations impose a heavy and constant strain on the mental powers. Nor is it inconsistent with dignity of character, or even with a certain austerity shown by those in official stations when thoroughly in earnest. One of the greatest magistrates who ever sat on the bench was occasionally so harsh in manner as to astonish as well as exasperate the bar, and, after metaphorically cuffing everybody he could reach, would go home — so the tradition goes — and romp with the children, playing "tag," or "catch as catch can," and dancing "till the gunpowder ran out of the heels of his boots."[1]

The anecdote is quite familiar of a famous theologian who was rolling on the floor with his grandchildren, and seeing through the window that a brother of the cloth was approaching the house, exclaimed: "Stop! there's a fool coming."

Those who attended the Φ. B. K. dinners at Cambridge forty years ago, when reporters were rigidly excluded, know very well how men of real distinction can play when they set out for a good time. The

[1] Those members of the bar who never saw the late Chief Justice Shaw, except in his regimentals and on the war path, may find it difficult to believe that at the bar-dinner given in honor of his appointment, about half a century ago, he sang the fine old melody of the "Unfortunate Miss Bailey." Still more difficult may be the belief, that, from diffidence or some error in the pitch, he fairly broke down! After the festivities had proceeded some time, he rose and said, "Mr. President, I move for a rehearing *in re Bailey*," which was granted amidst great applause.

loud, hilarious laughter of Judge Story, the classical hits of Everett, the keen edge of Judge Sprague's blade, the pithy points of Professor Parsons, the broad humor of Judge Warren, and the saturnine wit of Simon Greenleaf,[1] are things to be remembered.   It was Horne Tooke who declared that a " keen perception of the ludicrous is one of the greatest blessings of life."   Governor Andrew found it so, and the love of fun was a family trait.

It is something like thirty-five years since I was at the old Andrew homestead in Boxford.   They had organized a lyceum in the village, and Andrew was to deliver the

---

[1] When omnibuses were the only public conveyances between Cambridge and Boston, there was an old and big driver named Morse, whom everybody knew. At one of the Φ. B. K. dinners, Governor Kent of Maine was speaking of his gratification in coming back to the college, and especially that he found Morse still on top of his omnibus. Professor Greenleaf immediately cried out, " Mors est communis omnibus." Judge Story sprung to his feet and declared it the best impromptu thing he had ever heard at that table. But there was a report current among the outside barbarians that the Judge and Mr. Everett used to rehearse for these occasions.

opening lecture. It was an event in the town. The whole family with invited guests proceeded to the fearfully heated school-house, which was filled by an expectant crowd.

After a considerable delay, the presiding genius, whose mental and physical joints seemed never to have been unlimbered, arose, and with patronizing sternness addressed the orator of the evening thus: "*You may now begin.*" This was the whole introduction; and he did begin, while a broad smile illuminated his face at the sudden and remarkable manner in which he was precipitated upon the audience. After lecture, we drove home in the cold and bracing air, about as full of fun as mortals can be, and there spent an evening not easy to be forgotten. There was cider, the inevitable doughnuts, and all the Yankee "fixings," with a blazing fire that it is good to think about. What a time it was! What shouts of laughter at our own jokes! How we egged each other on for "more;" while Deacon Jonathan Andrew sat in the chimney-corner by himself, with his hand over his face, but the latter all aglow with the mirth he tried to conceal.

And the stories! I am not on oath, and may be mistaken as to which of them were told then and there. After passing the grand climacteric, these reminiscences of story-telling get slightly "mixed." It is almost a privilege of old age to repeat an anecdote — if it be a good one — to the same auditors, and none but an inconsiderate person will make known the fact, provided always that the narrator is of fair repute, and his tale is not very long, and is reasonably good. Nor is it quite fair for the young and handsome to remark of a story under such circumstances, that it was in the American Almanac forty years ago, or is as old as Faneuil Hall. Still less, to spoil the effect by alluding to a difference in the statement of facts in the present narration and one formerly made;

as, for instance, in calling the horse red now and formerly black. The precise color is not usually material.

One of the stories referred to I am sure of; for it was in the lecture, and related to good Parson Eaton, formerly of that parish. One of his church attributed his rare popularity to the fact that he never said anything in the pulpit about politics or religion! Then there was an account of the little girl who undertook to climb a high fence and fell. She was caught by her clothing until help came and she was rescued from her perilous condition. In speaking of her escape to a bachelor friend, the child concluded: " I should certainly have lost my life but for Providence, — and my drawers " !

Then there was the conversation between two little Sunday-school scholars: " There are two things," said one, " which I despise, — one is Sunday; the other is death." Here was an illustration of the possible value of a warm temper under peculiar circumstances. Parson Miltimore was " gifted in prayer," and was always relied upon to open county conferences and so forth. He got tired of it at length, and formally insisted that younger men should assume this duty. At the next meeting of the associated churches, he was purposely late. They waited for him, and he went up the pulpit stairs at a somewhat accelerated pace. After the prayer was over, a venerable brother remarked to him: " Brother Miltimore, you always pray well ; but never, I think, *so* well as when you are a little mad ! "

So, also, Parson Parrish of Byfield was greatly gifted in prayer. One remarkably pleasant Sunday, after a long drought, he prayed long and earnestly for rain. Soon after the services were ended, it began to rain to the great inconvenience of the good people, who had brought no umbrellas. Two farmers were hurrying along the road, thoroughly drenched, when one of them remarked : " Well, the minister certainly *is* powerful in prayer." "Yes," said the other testily, — shaking the rain from his coat, "*but he lacks judgment.*"

Then there was the incipient Governor's own account of the fugitive slave, whose Sunday-school teacher was instructing him in Bible history. He was greatly astonished at the story of Jonah in the whale's belly, but admitted that if it was in the good book it must be true. But, when told the next Sunday of Daniel in the lions' den, he declared that if *that* was in the same Bible, "darned if he believed the fish story now!"

Then there was the fighting parson, whom one of his parishioners asked to preach from Matthew v. 39: "Whosoever shall smite thee on thy right cheek turn to him the other also." "Certainly, he would the next Sunday." And there was a great crowd to hear how one of his temperament would treat such a subject. After giving out the text, he said the meaning was very clear and the doctrine satisfactory. " If a man smite thee on the right cheek, it may have been a mistake; it may have been in sudden passion and repented of at once. You should bear it and turn to him the other cheek in order to learn what his intention is. But if he smites you again, *let him have it;* for there is no Scripture against that!"

All this may be regarded by some as trifling, but to the sober-minded and sensible, anything which tends to illustrate the characteristics of this happy New England family, and the influences under which Governor Andrew passed his early youth, will be of interest in forming an estimate of his character and career. When an elaborate and adequate biography of this eminent magistrate is written, these peculiar traits must have their place.[1]

---

[1] Of Chief Justice Parsons, — who was denominated in his own day the *Giant of the Law*, and whom Mr. Justice Story once declared to be "a head and shoulders taller than any other man in the State," — his son and biographer says : " If ever any man loved fun and frolic, he did. He laughed easily and heartily, although often

His life was not an eventful one up to the time when the country was convulsed by civil war, and then the nation as well as individuals lived an age in a few years. In this grand drama he was a central figure, and never came short of public expectation in whatever position he was placed. The weaknesses and infirmities of the race were his, but when the time for *action* came, they disappeared to as great an extent as falls to the lot of humanity.

He was really a great man. His early negotiation of all the incongruous elements of Massachusetts society into a solid and powerful opposition to the South, so that

with his mouth shut and silently; he loved to laugh and to make others laugh, and knew how to do it. Nothing do I remember better than the hours of chat and laughter, — the very many such hours, — the gay dinners, the simple but festive suppers, which, as they come now before my recollection, seem to me full of unrestrained frolic. The fashion in that day was more tolerant of anecdote and fun of all kinds, in conversation and at all times, than it is now. Innumerable are the stories which have come to me of my father's sayings and doings in the way of jest, in all the periods of his life."

we had no discord at home, was a marvellous achievement. So was his courage marvellous in prohibiting the Federal government from arbitrary arrests in the Commonwealth till after the *Habeas Corpus* Suspension Act was passed. So was the influence marvellous which he exerted upon the country and upon the authorities at Washington, in clearly showing the true nature of the contest in which we were engaged, and in securing the adoption of the measures necessary for its successful termination; so was the sagacity he exhibited in making so few mistakes in the thousands of official appointments which were thrown upon him under new and trying circumstances; so was the magnanimity displayed in his valedictory address, considering the time when it was delivered.

Mr. Edwin P. Whipple, who was early selected as the most competent person to write the biography of Governor Andrew, and who to this end examined critically his whole private and official correspondence, of more than thirty thousand pages, declares to me that he could discover nothing in his most private notes which was not honorable. "Under the microscope nothing could be detected even when passions were raging the fiercest, which had the least taint of envy, jealousy, meanness, bigotry, or any unworthy feeling." The general impression he derived from looking over the whole correspondence was, that Governor Andrew "ranked among the purest, the most generous, the most magnanimous, the most unselfish and patriotic statesmen of the world."

At the same time, he was the most unconventional of men. He was simple in his tastes, natural in his appearance and conduct, and had a gentleness and a youthful artlessness of character united with a lion heart in courage.

> "His armor was his honest thought,
> And simple truth his utmost skill."

He passed more than twenty years in an arduous profession, and never earned more than enough for the decent and comfortable support of his family. He devoted his best years to the country, and lost his life in her service. His highest ambition was to do his duty in simple faith and honest endeavor. Of such a character the well-known lines of Sir Henry Wotton are eminently applicable : —

> "This man was free from servile bands
> Of hope to rise, or fear to fall ;
> Lord of himself, though not of lands,
> And having nothing, yet had all."

BURIAL-PLACE AND MONUMENT, HINGHAM, MASS.

ORATION

DELIVERED BEFORE THE

ATHENÆAN SOCIETY OF BOWDOIN COLLEGE.

SEPTEMBER, 1844.

ORATION.

Iᴛ has fallen to me, my brethren of the
Athenæan Society, to utter the words of
welcome, at this recurrence of our annual
festival.

Our Alma Mater has opened her arms
once more, and enfolds us now together
again, in the embrace of old and kindly
recollections, of warm and hearty greetings,
of young friendships matured or revived,
of manly and hopeful and generous faith
in each other and in our literary home.
Some of us are allowed to revisit her at
each return of our college thanksgiving;
some of us only meet around the family
board at longer intervals, to find the nurs-
lings, the children of the flock, grown
strong and stalwart men; to perceive the

lines deepening upon the countenances, and the locks growing thin and frosty on the brows of the elders; to witness how care and time and labor, how the toil of life, the burdens of the heart, the discipline of worldly conflict, how joy and sorrow, disappointment and success, health and disease, a quiet or a troubled spirit, have each left their traces behind them, marked on the cheek, in the expression of the eye, moulded into the frame, visible each in the port and bearing of the man; speaking each in the very tones of the voice.

But, whether seldom or frequent may be our mutual interviews, their great purpose and usefulness must be forever the same. Aside from the sympathies and finer senti- ments of the heart, which may and should be thus strengthened and protected; be- yond the awakening of emotions of min- gled sweetness and regret — far, oh, very far beyond the revisitings of early memo- ries, and the rekindling of early associations, is the *wisdom* that they may *teach* — the

wisdom, not merely nor mainly of thoughts
and opinions suggested by each others'
lips, but the wisdom of compared experience, the wisdom born of the reflections
the day will crowd upon us — the wisdom,
" uttered not, yet comprehended."

I know not what the introspection of
others may reveal to them. I doubt not,
however, that, with all the variety of circumstance, with all the peculiarity of temperament and character to be found among
us here, there are certain great, leading, and
distinctive impressions that belong to the
experience of us all. I speak now, rather
to my own cotemporaries, to the scholars
here met whose minds may be supposed to
have the most sympathy with my own, and
to whom I may, for all reasons, with the
more propriety, speak. There must be a
feeling, a conviction, that the world is somewhat different from the dream of the boy;
somewhat more real in its exactions; somewhat less so in its rewards. There must
be some plain and unrelenting facts, stand-

ing stiffly before the gaze of every one that
were quite unforeseen the morning that last
saw him joining the muster at early prayers
in the chapel. The bell that broke his slum-
bers and destroyed the visions of his sleep
was not more potent to dispel the sweet
creations of an untroubled mind, shut
out by kind forgetfulness from all thought
of care, than the " bell of time," as day by
day it has been sounding out the hours, has
proved its power to awaken the mind from
its repose of happy and confident anticipa-
tion, to scatter the well-woven plans of
hope, speculating blindfold, yet buoyant
and satisfied.

He has learned little from life to whom
the wrestling of a half dozen years against
the waves of that great and turbulent sea
into which the young man leaps so heartily,
when the days of his novitiate are over,
has not brought some new sense of duty,
of responsibility, and of obligation to the
time he lives in, the people among whom
he dwells, on account of which he must ask

for no compensation now, for the privilege of fulfilling which he must even give something himself. He has found, unless his life has been a blank, and his soul has existed shut in from all communion with the instructing testimonies of all events, both within and without himself, — that the mystery of life can find no solution; that the wants of his nature can find no corresponding good, that its struggles are the vain toil of a cheated mind; or else, he has learned, that he began to breathe the air of Heaven, and grew to man's estate, and studied books, and communed with men and nature, and pored over wearisome volumes, and read with eager eyes the pleasant ones, — that he recited lessons, and stood, day after day, chalk in hand, by a blackboard, marched solemnly to chapel, and skipped gladly to the commons; that he lived some certain years in a college, and, on a given day, received a puzzling parchment, with a ribbon and seal, from venerated hands, in a crowded meeting-house, with divers forms and ceremonies; that he has been styled by his neighbors, Reverend, or Doctor, or Esquire; that he has joined in the open and anxious competition of full grown men, on that broad arena of strife, where the earth is all unbounded before him, where mankind are his classmates and his competitors; that, in a word, he is *born* and *lives*, as one actor in a great and mysterious drama, the end of which is unrevealed, the control of which he holds not, the scenes of which are hourly changing, where all parts are assigned, where none may justly call himself *stage-manager* or *star*, but where each must act his part as he learns it on the stage, and forget himself in the character he plays.

I care not how great may have been the success, as we measure it in the street; I make no account of the brilliant rewards that a man may have been allowed to call his own: the result is as inevitable as the edict of death, that the scholar, perhaps more than most men, must find that there

is something to get which success does not
give him, something to gain, which the
rewards of wealth and eminence do not
command. The secret of it all is felt by
all men; it is understood and appreciated
by a few. Some facts are learned; but the
great doctrine they enfold is inoperative
upon the heart. We see it in the listless-
ness and discouraged inactivity of one who
has found life harder, and success more
difficult than he dreamed it in his college
visions. We see it in the unsatisfied countenance and murmured complaint of
another, whose march has been triumph
over all those misfortunes which we fear
the most, into whose lap plenty has
poured the contents of her horn, and upon
whose brow fame has bound her laurels.
We see it all over society, in the pages of
unhopeful books and newspapers; in the
light and hard habits of money-getting, in
that notable absence of hearty enthusiasm
that makes our lives.

I do not speak in the language of complaint. I look upon the world with no distempered eye, — but the *truth*, known to us all, may well enough be confessed. It is worth the utterance, for it points to something which is no misfortune in nature. It is the witness of something great, lofty, and elevating in duty, in capacity, and in destiny, which, when perceived and grasped, shall be the cure of what is wrong, the creator of a new order in the individual and in society.

It is the highest office of scholarship to observe what is, and to inquire what ought to be. Whoso has any other philosophy has not read, as yet, the title-page of that mysterious volume the Almighty has placed in his hands, the leaves of which are turned over, whether he will or no, before his face, open to his study, inviting his care. And in the few suggestions which I shall have the honor now, with great deference to submit, connected mainly with the position of the younger class of our brethren, touching the practical aims of

American scholars, I shall assume its *truth.*

What is the existing position of our young men as they embark on their voyage for life, — masters of themselves, — and what should it be ? With what views and purposes, and in what pursuit do they commence and prosecute their enterprise ? and what exchange do they propose to themselves in return for the argosies they bear off upon the seas? If I were to give a name to the greatest cause of evil to the individual, and of inefficiency to his influence in the world, for all good and noble things, that now pervades the ranks of American scholars, — by which I mean all those to whom courtesy grants the title, — I should call it, *the want of a devoted enthusiasm.*

The character of later times, — the whole tone of the thrifty and calculating civilization of the nineteenth century, has contributed not a little to divest every pursuit and all the vocations of society of that *free* and *hearty* and *generous self-forgetfulness*, upon which the birth of great enterprises, and the accomplishment of mighty and brilliant deeds, that alone give to the world a history, depend no more than the moral elevation and private happiness of every individual man. We labor to live, and we live to labor. To buy and to sell; to increase our store; to swell our comforts and to enlarge our wealth, is the nation's struggle and the people's toil. Not to say, that in these things, even, we are more selfish than our grandfathers; this better outward man; these fairer fields; these palaces of luxury, and these frequent dwellings of competence and ease, have taught forgetfulness of hard and rugged days when men suffered and denied themselves, that they might earn all this for us. We are in advance of our fathers in a thousand things. Nay, the world has grown wiser, and better, too, I doubt not, in every step of its procession, — but the very advantages that old experience has given us; the very con-

quests that time and effort have made for
the race over sin and folly, have brought
with them new necessities and fresh perils
for society. The simple and inartificial
relations of men to each other, have given
way to the elaborate and more involved
connections of greater wealth, higher intellectual culture, and an advanced social
condition. The heart and the life of the
young scholar feels this want of enthusiasm, as an element of social life, more than
he knows, infinitely more than I can tell.
His aims are controlled by it, his profession
is selected by it, his mode of life grows up
under it, and his influence, — his influence, — that which is at once his wealth and
his responsibility, is warped and enfeebled,
and but too frequently perverted by it.

We hear much of a generous spirit of
emulation, but we hear little of the highest
ambition. It is everywhere held that one
should, if possible, out-do his neighbor, but
how little do we feel that we should make
the most of ourselves. Our life is indi-

vidual self-interest carried out, almost to
the last analysis. And though we can present the spectacle of a wonderful progress
as compared to the days when myriads
lived for the glory of a monarch, when the
man was the victim of the State, when there
were no citizens, but only serfs and soldiers; yet these conditions had their rec-
ompense, to which we must and shall
have something to correspond, without
which our progress is only outward and
superficial. The difference is a great one
in degree, but not very remarkable or
prominent in kind between the barbarian
who gives up his will and his conscience
to a despotic leader, and follows, in blind
submission, the standard of a warrior chief,
and risks himself upon the field of stricken
battle, to gain his portion in the spoils of
war; and the free citizen, who boasts of
his right of suffrage, and the independent
tenure of his lands, but thinks it right
to lie down before an unsanctified public
opinion, for the sake of what, by such good

policy, he may make out of the unsuspicious and the feeble.

The subject of a despotism, in a dark age, with all his indifference to the tender and the humane, is excited and stimulated to no insignificant degree of manly ardor, by the mere sentiment of loyalty — one which long outlives the decays of time and often survives the structures of Reform. There is the blind enthusiasm, too, of patriotism, that leads men of some periods and nations to cast to the winds fortune, life, and even glory itself, for the sake of their country. There is the pride of the clan, the rivalship of states, there is zeal for some form of religious faith, a burning desire to witness the triumph of something, to which the heart has been wedded, to gain which, no sacrifices are deemed too costly. How the spirit leaps within us, as we read the stories of bravery and self-devotion, which have created the fame of heroes, and made bad enterprises romantic, and bad men respectable. These forms of social life that wheel the mass around some central head, whether it be the monarch, the hero, or something more abstract; and those states of society in which personal prowess and defiance of personal danger are counted high among the virtues of a man, in training them to live and act zealously for something entirely apart from private acquisition, — build up an element of enthusiasm, in a people's character, that fits them for great emergencies, and furnishes the nation with an invincible spirit for the pursuit of any good the people may have wisdom enough to work for; while, on the other side, the elevation in political rights, and in social importance, of all the classes of society, while it does no more than justice to the individual, does as much, in one view of the matter, to refine upon human selfishness, as it does to vindicate the claims of the subject against the encroachments of the despot or the state. In just so far as this progress is the fruit of generous devotion to principles, with the truth and beauty of which we have become enamored, in just so far do we escape the evil: but, when we lose sight of the ideal, the abstract; when we fight for a principle, only for its application to ourselves,—in just so far do we degrade ourselves, and tend to perpetuate human wrongs under altered forms and with fresher strength. The tendency to elevate the individual and the tendency to extreme utilitarianism, as they always move side by side with each other, making selfishness in every man's bosom a kind of resulting force out of the two, are and have been, during the nineteenth century, acting strongly in concert, moulding and controlling its civilization. And though the rectifying causes are also at work, it is only too plain that those parts of society that succeed in getting the most advantage from existing institutions are quite too careless of their brethren, and feel all too much their own individual importance to labor any farther than what a good worldly policy counsels, for the final triumph of all the interests of humanity. I admit that there is much downright love of principle, and much hearty labor, both here and abroad, for the good of man ; but the idea of *utility* is, for the sake of utility itself, too much at the bottom of it all, and reform of the grosser abuses prevails but little faster than the political economists can be convinced that the public wealth will be increased by it the next year ; and the craftsman, the tradesman, the merchant, and the speculator can feel safe from any possible danger to prices or derangement to the markets. From the man that digs his living out of an oyster-bed, to the capitalist who lolls from ten o'clock in the morning till dinner time in insurance offices and at directors' boards, and eats his dinner till sundown and digests it when he can, and so up and down, through all the gradations of social life between the two, does this worshipping of utility prevail. In one country you must do nothing which will, by any possibility, disturb the three estates of the realm; in another you must hold still, lest you have the royal prerogative; or, if no other evil *can* be feared, then he must be quiet lest he frighten the royal children; while, here at home, we have to dodge where we can, in order to preserve the influence of our political party, our religious denomination, or to prevent the shaking of some outward institution profanely styled an ark of safety. The safest way for all moralists and states-men, too, is to imitate the sagacious caution of the clergyman of whom it was said by his deacon that he was the pattern of min-isters, as he never meddled with politics or religion in the pulpit.

It is well that a spirit of rugged inde-pendence should hold its unshaken seat in the breast of every freeman; that he should look out well that none should rob him of his bread, or of his chance of gain-ing it. It would be a noble thing if every man would refuse to vote for a measure, until convinced by facts and reasoning;

but it would be infinitely nobler and better
if he would always vote, accordingly, when
convinced that a measure is right, instead
of waiting to find whether it will be popular or politic.   Some things must be taken
for granted: they must be believed *a pri-
ori;* and, without that, you destroy all the
freshness and beauty of goodness, and all
the vitality of faith.   If you break loose
from loyalty, and dethrone your king, you
must fall back upon patriotism, and act
under love of country, as your ruling sentiment; if you outgrow that, and value your
country for what it gives you, and think it
hard to fight her battles unless you eat her
bread, then you must take a step higher
than patriotism, unless you would descend
to one even lower than loyalty, and must
become a philanthropist; you must love
your neighbor as yourself, and find a neighbor wherever you find a man.   I bring no
railing accusation against this era when I
say that the principle of loyalty and the
sentiment of patriotism as mere unreason-

ing impulses have grown less and less; while the wider sentiment, that true and more noble impulse of philanthropy, has failed to approach quite so fast as they have receded. Apply, if you choose, the test. Will a man do and suffer as much for his neighbor as the subject would have done for his liege? Will the voice of humanity plead as effectually in our hearts, as would our country's call, even in these calculating times? Will it stir them up to deeds of self-devotion, and make us glad to live or count it glorious to die to vindicate the wrongs of others?

Say, is it not true that, as you hear less and less of the trumpet's *music*, you feel less and less of that ardent, impulsive, and glowing fervor of soul, in which the great and brave of every age have forgotten fear, despised self-interest, and abandoned themselves in a cause?

Out of this intense individualism grows a narrow, personal ambition, that breeds much of the failure to be found in our

learned professions.   As the field is open
to all, we go, each alone, into the conflict,
and we fight, each man for himself.   The
success of one is not merged in the success
of many,—in the triumph of any particular
banner: he has no standard by whose fate
his own is to be determined; no leader
whose waving plume is his own bright ori-
flamme.   No dread of common danger, no
hope of united glory, link our hearts together, save our political parties, and our
religious sects, and our philanthropic societies, our interest in which forms, after all,
but a mere trifling infusion of sentiment
and motive compared to the entire compo-
sition of our ruling purposes: we *live* and
toil and *die* alone.   If, in surveying the
ground upon which our energies are to be
expended, we see no bristling array of
forces standing, in regular battle order, to
meet and oppose our advance, neither do
we see a host of fellow-soldiers, who greet
our accession to their ranks with welcome cheers.   The only remedy, and it is

one which, to a good extent, the recupera-
tive energies of the race are constantly
supplying — the result towards which the
whole course of Providence is pointing —
which is the genius of the Christian religion, is the modification of all forms of
antagonism and combat, and the substitu-
tion, in their stead, of an universal union.
In that result, is the great destiny of scholarship to be realized, and towards the production of it must genius and learning
and the highest gifts of human culture contribute. The young man must abandon
the mere purpose of personal distinction.
If he lives for himself, all the chances are
against his realizing the dreams of his ambition; if he prevails, he has not purchased
contentment and peace, though he has expended all the wealth of his being.

Do not imagine me, while I advocate a
spirit of enthusiasm, to commend fanati-
cism; while I would fix some limits to individual self-concern, to strike at individual
liberty or effort; while I believe in some-

thing nobler than utility, to connive at recklessness; while I would check self-conceit, to neglect wisdom. I would have enthusiasm, thoughtful and considerate; I would have philanthropy begin at the individual, as the centre of a circle, and radiate outward to the remotest circumference of humanity; and I would have devotedness to the highest theories practically applied; I would have that wisdom, of which it was said by the son of Sirach, "She is more moving than any motion; for she passeth, and goeth through all things, by reason of her pureness. For she is the breath of the power of God, and a pure influence flowing from the glory of the Almighty; therefore, can no defiled thing fall into her. For she is the brightness of the everlasting light, the unspotted mirror of the power of God, and the image of his goodness. And being but one she can do all things, and, remaining in herself, she maketh all things new, and in all ages, entering into holy souls, she maketh them friends of God and prophets."

I contend for those motives and forms of action, which, while they shall never fetter the activity of the higher sentiments of the intellectual and spiritual being, shall do no wrong to what we call common sense and practical skill.

The genuine man, who feels the worth of life, is illustrated somewhat to my mind by the brave and gallant general. He does not march out, by himself, in sheer recklessness of what darts and rifle-balls can do; he does not stand, for the sake of proving his temerity, upon an open eminence, and challenge all the marksmen of the foe to hit him, if they can; but when the hordes of Xerxes are pouring down for conquest, and some one must command the pass at Thermopylae, there he goes, and there he stands, in spite of every peril, the leader of the *forlornest hope.*

Such have always been the philosophers, the reformers, the teachers, the heroes of the race. Socrates had no ambition to die by hemlock; but rather than embrace the casuistry of the Sophists, — rather than abandon his teachings, or compromise the virtues of his character, — he drained the poison, and closed his eyes forever. Luther was not in love with the rigors of collision with the tremendous power of Rome; but as his awakened spirit led him through storm and trial, on his road to the fulfilment of Truth and Duty, he cast aside all fear of man and defied the Vatican.

> " Half-battles were the words he said,
>   Each born of prayer, baptized in tears,
> And routed by him, backward fled
>   The errors of a thousand years."

So, too, Lafayette, that bright example of the most generous and hearty and glorious enthusiasm in modern political history ; think you that the gifts of fortune, rank, and domestic bliss, which, all combined, lacked the power to chain him to the soil of France, while the voice was echoing in his ears, — think you that all these had no charm for him? But, though gifted with a moderation that frowned upon all excesses, with a calm self-command that was never moved, though liberty tempted to license, and zeal was transformed, in other minds, to fury, he spurned them all, to be the friend and soldier of Washington. How full of meaning and of consolation are histories such as these! How do they vindicate the right and exalt virtue, and justify principle! Who is there so drunk and mad with the idea of momentary glory, — who is there, whose low ambition, satisfied with the gewgaws of an hour, would not rather be Lafayette than Napoleon? Who would buy the imperial throne on which the *Man of Destiny* sat his day, and exchange for it that lofty seat in the gratitude of two nations, and in the admiration of the world, won by Lafayette, in a life of self-sacrifice and devotion to his principles? Nay, judging by any worldly standard merely, was it more glorious to tumble from the giddy height of unjust dominion, and die a prisoner and an exile upon a rock in the sea, than to have lingered in the dungeon of Olmutz, a captive and a martyr to Liberty, with the protecting sympathies of mankind for a support, to come forth, at last, to a higher and prouder triumph than this world ever saw before, and to guide the destinies of his dear France in her next hour of trial? One more great and immortal spectacle of the enthusiasm I defend was exhibited in the pilgrimage of the Plymouth Puritans: I mean no disparagement to the devotedness of others, — to any of the examples of modern heroism, that the earlier history of our continent presents, — but there are few stories in the annals of mankind so pathetic, so heroic, as theirs. When we compare the feebleness of their resources, the insignificance of their numbers, their poverty and isolated condition, both from the helps and sympathies of the world, with their unconquerable zeal, their meek submission, their bold and undaunted energy, and their humble and trusting piety; when we contrast their first impressions upon the tablets that

record the doings of the race with the results that have followed the landing of the
" Mayflower," — we may well pause, in our
careers of selfishness, and gain strength
from their exemplary lesson in the majesty
of enthusiastic virtue. Oh! was not that
a great landmark on the coast of time, when
the *benignant and faithful Carver*, the *venerable, gray-headed Brewster*, the *dignified
and amiable Bradford*, the *youthful and
gifted Winslow*, the great heart of manhood, the holy truth of woman's love and
childhood banished from the soft lap of
home, standing on a lonely rock, on a
savage shore, their hopes on Heaven, the
martyrs of conscience, the founders of a
state, triumphant over all dismay,

> " They shook the depths of the desert gloom
> With their hymns of lofty cheer."

The youthful and aspiring scholar finds
little in our communities to encourage him
to imitate histories such as these. That
part of society with which he has the readi-
est contact, and whose influence he feels

the most, are quite too comfortable, their carpets are too soft, their suppers too good, and their ideas too much governed by " the main chance " to encourage the free scope of his ardor. If he would not accept a good call; if he would not marry a rich wife, with a good opportunity; if he would not keep quiet about any odd notions he held, rather than risk a loss or patronage,— how many there are in society, who would doubt whether what he exhibited as his degree were not the certificate that ought to carry him to the lunatic asylum instead of an academical diploma !

This age has, nevertheless, a larger sympathy with the advance guard of progress; for the leaven of Christian morals has more thoroughly penetrated it. But, when was there a time that the very institutions of government and society did not provide for and encourage that very impulse in human nature of which we are speaking ? There has been the cloister, or the convent, for one; there has been the distant pilgrimage for another; the wearing penance and the midnight vigil for a third. And there has been war, in all its fascinating pomp and crime, with its elegant amenities occasionally relieving its unnatural barbarities, — the field and the camp, for the realization of many a vision of glory.

But, passing from this branch of the subject, let me explain what I mean by what should be the aims and pursuits of the American scholar, — the mode in which he must be at once enthusiastic and practical. He must be a man of thought and of deep convictions. A man *is* what he believes, —he is the embodiment of what he feels to be true, — the living witness and exemplar of his faith. I do not undertake to point out his creed, but only to say, that he must believe *something*, and act as if he believed it to be true. He must not be a bigot; but he has no right to be a doubter. He must be open to new convictions, and to the modification of old ones; but he must find some great principles which are ever permanent, and judge his opinions by these as his standards.

He must look with a grateful countenance upon the past, but he must look with hope upon the future. "We are not," says one of the leading minds of our country, "to hand down the world just as we found it." This idea should possess itself of every American scholar; and he should seek to learn what duty it assigns to *him.* The men who gave immortal renown to the 4th July in 1776, did not believe that all human wisdom and prowess could do for human liberty was exhausted some five hundred years before, when the British barons wrested from the reluctant John, at Runnymede, the great forest charter of British rights; and forthwith they framed a declaration of independence. The founders of our government thought well, no doubt, of the famous edict of Nantes, by which, under the first Bourbon, the gallant Henry of Navarre, the bleeding and

hunted Huguenots found a period of repose
from the pangs of persecuting zealots ; but
they still believed it to be reserved for
themselves to frame a republican constitution. They were masters of the thought,
that to every time belongs a duty and a
destiny.

But the tendency of our minds is now
quite largely towards the belief that the
days for heroism are over. The belief is
not universal. It is not true, and it will
not last. There *is* yet to be an era of
moral heroism that shall challenge, by its
devotedness, the best days of the martyrs;
and it shall be unstained by blood, uncon-
trolled by worldly policy. It shall carry
no sword but truth, no torch but the light
of its own bright influence. It shall bring
no tears but those of penitence ; it shall
break no ties but those of bondage. It is
the duty of the scholar to perceive and to
know the signs of his age. He is bound
to sympathize with its wants and to stand
a sentinel upon its watch-towers. He has

no right to repose under the shadows of
the past; to eat his bread and drink his
wine; and take, listlessly, the goods that
fortune has provided for him.   He has
been favored by communion with the
minds of sages and philosophers; he has
drank from the wells of science; he has
furnished himself from the records of human experience, and has established, by
the aid of books and reflection, a mysterious telegraphic union between the thought
and the history of the past, and his own
soul.   But the philosophers did not think
for him only.   Sages did not write merely
to fill his mind with truth; the poets have
not sung, to give him, only, the music of
their lays; history was not written for the
amusement of his study: the sufferings
and the triumphs of humanity have no
restricted office.   The true scholar is the
servant of his neighbors: he is bought with
a price; he is paid by the best wealth of
all ages, of which he has collected a part,
whose storehouses he cannot exhaust, and

from which he may gather without hin-
derance.

It is no arrogance to assert that, were
the aims of all our young men who become yearly candidates for the learned
professions sufficiently single and well-
directed, not only would the standard of
excellence in them all be immeasurably
elevated, but the prosperity, the happiness,
and the moral tone of society itself would
be renewed. Who does not know what an
amount of power (all the more efficient,
because voluntarily bestowed) rests always
in their hands ; how they teach weekly
in our pulpits, and how widely their opinions are respected; how they control our
schools and universities; how they are
heard by our firesides, in our caucuses and
conventions ; how they act through the
press ; how they crowd our halls of legislation, and sit upon our benches of justice.
Were they educated, and gifted with all
these means of influence and power, only
that they might gain a living, and be written

of in the newspapers? The Indian hunter
gets the first, by chasing buffaloes and trap-
ping game.   A juggler or a rope-dancer
will make more of a figure in print than
they can.   The elegant author may be
noticed in the magazines; but the man
who can ride four horses at once, without a
saddle or a bridle, will stare at you, in mam-
moth capitals, from every corner of the high-
way.   The writer of a useful book may walk
through Broadway or Washington Street,
and ten men shall not know him; but
a nimble *figurante* will be cheered by a
crowded theatre.   But you say that your
influence and respectability among your
neighbors is beyond all comparison with
rewards like these.   And why?   If you
value fame so highly, why not do that by
which you may get before the largest
number in the quickest way?   If you are
anxious to be rich, why not learn to perform an Ethiopian dance better than any
artiste now on the boards, and make your
fortune at once by it?   The answer is

ready: We want not cheers; we want respect: we seek not notoriety; we would have an honest fame: we don't care to be stared at as *curiosities;* we wish to be honored as *men:* we value ready cash; but we would get it by some worthy and useful means.

Then there is something better than applause,—something richer than gold. I accept the doctrine: and I ask that the objects of pursuit among American scholars shall be placed higher than the highest merely conventional excellence; that its rewards shall be measured by their absolute worth, and not by their price in the market.

There must always be some who are advocates of opinions in advance of their neighbors, of society in general. Until the world has grown old, and until mankind has "burnt out," and this round earth has become useless as a place of discipline, there must be the desire for change, — the thirst for realizing a higher life, in the forms and institutions of society. You cannot help it if you would. You would contradict all the purposes of the race, if you did. This fact the scholar should comprehend and feel, and of it let him never be afraid. He should avail himself of its advantages, and help to give tone and direction to the movement spirit of his time. He should study the tides of human thought; he should watch the breezes of human impulse; he should fathom those mysterious undercurrents of life upon which society is forever borne onward. Its life-principle is Truth, and *Truth* should be the bright object of his devotion. He should be its hearty student and its faithful witness. But " let none imagine," says the most eloquent and profound of American essayists, — " let none imagine that its chosen temple is an uncultivated mind, and that it selects as its chief organs the unlearned. It is indeed appointed to carry forward mankind; but not as concerned and expounded by narrow minds, not as darkened by the ignorant, not as debased by the superstitious, not as subtilized by the visionary, not as thundered out by the intolerant fanatic, not as turned into drivelling cant by the hypocrite. It requires for its full reception, and powerful communication, a free and vigorous intellect." All that is generous and expansive in learning, all that is profound and sublime in philosophy, should be seized anxiously by the scholar, and contributed to the work of progress. If he neglects his own cultivation, and does not strive to master all the problems and assist in the development of whatever truth may bear practically upon the interests of society, think you that the debt he owes can ever be repaid? Let him not suppose that the discussion of vexing and dangerous topics will cease, because the more educated are in general silent upon them. It cannot be. No cry comes up from the wilderness, that does not proceed from some precursor of good. It behooves him to listen to and to catch

the first intimation of movement, — to find
out from what point it starts; to learn
what is its basis, in the real wants of humanity, and to co-operate with all earnest
minds, in giving to it efficiency and usefulness. Let him be silent, and the very
stones will cry out for him. Let the pulpit be dumb, when human sin is the
subject, the ministers of religion will be
denounced as the ministers of Satan, and
the altars of the Christian faith will be
avoided as the altars of Belial. Let the
statesman speak peace, when there is none;
let him deprecate unwelcome discussion
of questions intricate in statesmanship and
troublesome in national affairs; let him
avoid the issues that time and the evolu-
tions of events have made up for him: and,
while he is tampering with the people's
patience and trying to make policy look
like principle, he will find that the hasty
and the excited will break loose, and even
the cool and self-controlled will become
inflamed; and they will curse him, and his

policy, and the constitution itself together. But let him have faith enough in the truth and in man to suffer no covert motives to control his public conduct, and he will learn that the old Hibernianism, that " the best way to avoid danger is to *face it plump*," is not the paradox it may seem.

I think that one error is about old enough now to be abandoned. I mean the idea that so conveniently associates the theorist with the marplot, and commends the mere tactician as your truly practical man. There is surely nothing worthy a scholarlike mind in this. It has no philosophy in it, and, of consequence, no wisdom or truth. It is a popular idea in party politics, but it is one against which our young men should plant themselves forever. If you have no theory, you have no plan; and if you have no plan, you have no thought, and can be governed by no definite purpose. It has prevailed so much, both at home and abroad, in affairs of state, that the most stupid barrenness has often imposed its jugglery upon the people, and called it sagacious policy. Look at the two great political parties in England, for example. How little do the great principles at the bottom of the two find themselves consistently applied by the party leaders. The Tory contents himself with preserving the ancient forms, and is consoled by the mummy of an old institution, after he has suffered the life to die out of it; while the reforming Whig is silenced by a mere piece of political mechanism which will wear out in the using.

The best hopes of enlightened conservatism and of national reform, whether it be in politics or morals, grows from the same parent stock. And the mistiness that shades the opinions, the uncertainty that paralyzes the efficiency, of parties would be no longer the reproach of so many public organizations, were there more of that far-reaching sagacity, furnished by well-considered principles, steadily adhered to. Men would understand each other better, would find less that they doubted in each other's motives, as they saw each other's doctrines the more clearly, and would build up a mutual respect, when they learned to comprehend this faith. They would find a solid basis for discussion, grow less bigoted as to measures; nay, they would unite in theory where they now believe themselves to differ.

The true scholar is the apostle of Hope; his voice is like that of the great-hearted Lars Anders in that splendid romance so full of truth and natural pathos which has lately come to us from the North.

"Yes, I will preach of Hope; I will speak of it in dungeons and prisons; I will shout it in the ears of the dying malefactor; I will sound it to the other side of death. I will cry into boundless eternity, Hope ye, hope ye!"

But Hope is not blind. It hopes because it perceives a prospect; or, rather, we hope because of what we see and know,—because of a deep foundation in truth, upon which hope sits naturally, smiling and secure.

He, then, who would be a useful friend to his country must be a thorough and brave student of principles, upon which alone policy can find a basis, which alone can furnish to hope a permanent foundation. Anybody can be an alarmist, a croaker. We never need to send abroad for Balaams to curse our Israel: we have a plenty of such prophets with no inspiration. But we need wise men, to whom a present mist shall not appear an endless night; who shall not torment us with evil forebodings, because of some momentary exigency, and scare us out of our comfort and our growth at every eclipse of the moon. We want statesmen to whom those mighty laws are familiar, those invisible powers are known, by which the world is controlled and human destiny evolved; who shall not mistake the tides for a flood, the beautiful and conservative eccentricities of nature for dissolution of the world.

In what I say of the influence and responsibility of the learned professions, I mean to make no assumptions on the one hand, no comparisons, invidious, on the other. I mean, however, to insist strenuously upon the great duty of their members to make their peculiar advantages of position the means of promoting the widest good. You must be true to your own mind, or you cannot be true to human nature. If you do not respect yourself and your own convictions, you have no reverence worth the bestowing for others. If you do not stand by the rights of the individual mind, represented in yourself, you are untrue to man, and faithless to the universal heart of humanity. There is no bondage worse than the spiritual slavery of the few to the majority; and there is nothing more useless or more cowardly. It is, after all, no compliment to majorities to pretend to be convinced when the votes are counted against you. Public opinion is made up of individual convictions. If you must yield your convictions to the public, every other man must, when the vane changes, relinquish his also, and thus all the value of public sentiment is destroyed. It becomes a weathercock and phantom. It is one thing to submit gracefully when you are beaten, but it is quite another to run away without a fight. He is unfit to be the object of popular regard who bows to the dictation of old authority or to the voice of the people, until he is convinced by reasons before which his mind naturally gives way. Let every man, of whatever capacity, be *free;* and the aggregate mass makes a free people : nor can you compose a body of freemen from any different materials; you can make freedom in no other way. It is an insult to the people to tell them they are always right; nobody will believe you, if you do. Every man knows himself to be sometimes wrong. No man places implicit confidence in the infallibility of his neighbors, and the doctrine of the infallibility of the people can find no basis in the practical sense of mankind. Moreover, individuals change; and as they go over from one side to another, so majorities sway from one extreme in the arc of opinion to the opposite: so that, this deference to majorities, if it were not the boldest, hollowest flattery, would be the most contemptuous and impudent sarcasm. As one of the people myself, I say that we are oftener wrong than otherwise, and so we have the right to be.

There is, also, an opposite condition of mind with which one may any day come in contact, — a perverse unbelief in anything but forms and institutions. There are not a few to whom a constitutional government is still a mere experiment, — to whom republicanism seems almost like stealing the thunder from Jupiter. Nothing looks safe and natural that does not trudge along under the protection of crown and mitre. All generous impulse, and everything hearty and spontaneous, is frightful and disorganizing.

The American scholar should stand equally far from those sycophantic fawners upon the multitude, and these scared children of dusty traditions. The present should be his stand-point; he may gather wisdom from every age, but the future is inevitable. There he is bound, there he must go. He cannot retard the car of time; let him beware how he clogs the wheels of human progress by his superstitions on the one hand or his demagogism on the other. Let him hold fast the maxim of a great and a contemplative mind, "*Progress*, the growth of power, is the end and boon of liberty." Combining individual independence of thought with reverence for the rights of all minds; enthusiasm and true devotion to his own faith with practical sagacity, he will learn to make scholarship something more than picking the dry bones of antiquated lore, he will find in it the means of comprehending and reproducing the living thoughts it expresses and preserves. Something better than the stepping-stone to popular distinction — he will make it the *Servant of*

Truth. And wherever his lot is cast in life, — whatever his sphere of control, — he will help to build up in the people a deeper faith, more profound and abiding convictions, a frank and self-possessed independence, the freest and heartiest toleration. And wherever one may be found whose purposes and efforts have an elevation like this, *him* do I hail as the true, the model scholar. He may have earned no reputation among men, for the variety or singularity of his learning; he may have shrunk, always, from the blaze of public positions, nor tempted the dangerous highways that lead to fame; he may be no book-maker, no poet, no orator, but he is better than all these if he is an honest searcher for the truth, and the faithful witness of what he knows. He is the genuine scholar, inspired by the true enthusiasm. He is the practical man, the benefactor of the people. He is strengthened by all good influences, and resists, with equal vigor, the seductions of ease and the alluring bait of ambition.

The *man* stands before the *scholar*. Say what we will of high attainments, of distinguished position, of professional eminence ; exalt and defend learning and literature and science, as you will; let it be forever remembered that none of these, nor all these combined, can make a MAN. They may be added *to* a man, but they are not *him*.

> All these may be the " guinea's stamp,
> The *man's* the gold, for a' *that*."

Indeed, in this country, it can hardly be, that there are any who may, as a class, in strictness — and by comparison with the rest of the world — be called scholars. Learning is too widely diffused to allow the mantle of scholarship to settle down upon the shoulders of any given order in society. Our best scholars are not always the bearers of professional or literary titles, and those who have them are not always scholars. Let us be grateful that it is so. Learning *should* be like genius, having no intimation of any aristocracy. It should go to *human nature,* unmindful of accident or circumstance; as the sweet muse of poetry visits alike the peasant Burns, toiling on the cold and rugged heaths of Scotland, and the youthful and titled Byron, bearing the honors of a noble house. The highest intellectual culture, to be availing, must develop the *man.* You may hang about yourself all the ornaments that artifice can devise, you may trick out your scholarship with all the best finery of learning, you may become the admiration of artists and the wonder of the unskilful, — but, stopping there, you will have done nothing that the world will thank you for, nothing for gratitude, nothing for memory. But plant deep in the foundations of eternal truth, educate and bring out all within you, by which you are united in the great sympathies of a common nature and a common destiny, with the loftiest and the comeliest of the human brotherhood, *and you shall not die.* You shall live in grateful hearts after the proudest monumental marbles have crumbled away. You shall erect for yourself a memorial of joy that will be sweet to you in the declivity of years, and shall comfort you, " in the travail of mortality."

Faith! faith in man and faith in God; this, this is the secret of true enthusiasm. It is this which has embalmed thought, and given immortality to genius. Go where you will, to all literatures, whether of Christendom or of Heathendom, and there you will find it so. Where is the cynic, the doubter, the sceptic, who has contrived to grapple to himself the hearts of men? He may have glittered in the courts of princes, he may have shone in the saloons of gayety, but the humblest believer in *any* religion, the untrumpeted worshipper of any thing divine is more noble and more beloved. Scepticism and unbelief in those great ideas, moulded now into one, and now into another form of religious faith, have no place in the literature that has come to us from those who have found the master-key to human hearts, who have marshalled the progressive tread of ages. But religion has given to the productions of those who have drawn inspiration from her sacred fountains, the leaven of eternal truth, and has imparted to them of her own eternity. Here let us rest at last. Christianity, the true, the perfect, the last revelation to the human soul, makes her commanding appeal to us all, as men, and as scholars. And we are *feeble* as well as *false* if we refuse to bow down before her. To what purpose is culture if it rise not above the earth we tread upon? Of what avail is learning if we are ignorant of that science, toward which all philosophy has been struggling, and of which Christianity is the teacher?

Let the lips of the orator be touched with a living coal from off the altar of the Lord. Let the poet breathe the airs of Palestine, once vocal with the music and the harp of David; let the philosopher be instructed by the profound metaphysics of

Paul; let the whole man be purified by the simple, the sublime revelation of the Gospel. We may do something then, but not otherwise. For power, and learning, and wisdom, and eloquence can do nothing alone. A man with leather-girdled loins will come up from the wilderness, and wake the slumbering echoes of all Judea, and the heartless formalist, the wily Pharisee, and the learned rabbi shall tremble before him. For God can choose the weak things of the world to confound the strong, and foolish things of the world to con. found the wise; aye, and things that are not, to set at nought the things that are.

ADDRESS

AT THE CLOSE OF THE SCHOOL YEAR

OF THE

MAINE FEMALE SEMINARY.

GORHAM, JULY, 1859.

ADDRESS.

Five-and-twenty years have enrolled themselves on the records of the irrevocable past since I — in all the inexperience and trembling hope of early boyhood — passed out of the portals of what was then known, widely and honorably known, as the Gorham Academy, to join my class in the wider sphere and maturer studies of the college. From the single, intellectual and moral guidance of that noble-hearted and kindly-stern old man, whose earnest eye and deep-toned voice, and whose figure, bent by too absorbing devotion to his work and books, are among the ineffaceable memories of a life-time; hence I departed, no more to come again, save as a pious pilgrim to a shrine, where linger tender and holy recollections, winning back the willing feet of manhood to stand awhile in love and reverence where once they danced in the earlier years.

I look upon the well-known faces and dwellings of the village, and recognize the features of a familiar landscape, preserved in the eye not only by the force of their original impression, but as retouched by now and then a flying visit and a hasty summary and survey of their changes. The walks, the play-grounds, the daily ascent to school, the quiet nooks, where friendly trees defended us from the summer's sun, the very dust of summer and the snow-drifts of the winter, as well as the dear companions of those innocent and more careless days, — some whose friendship during all these years has rendered life more worth the living, and some whose memories make the " silent land " itself fragrant and beautiful, — come back with me to-day, and we seem to re-visit together and to hold a fond reunion.

The intervening years become a dream; so many seasons, with their birds and fruits; so many storms and so many fertilizing showers; so many experiences of life and death; of hope and disappointment; so many heavy hours, when the flesh was weary and the whole head sick; so many strong and gallant days when we stood up in the current of the heady fight, when the battle-axe was but a feather, for heart and hand were both so strong; so many forebodings have been unrealized and so many mercies have been spent; the fathers have passed away and their sons have grown gray with years and cares. And, yet, as the river sweeping by leaves no trace upon its banks of sand, as the ripple melts away into the mirrored surface of the pool, as the earth — mother of us all — is young and shows no scars of time, so does the benignant Providence smooth down the roughness of our lives, tempering all things by such merciful adjustment, that the aged heart is warm and the heart of manhood is fresh with youth. I look about upon the fathers and upon those, my own cotemporaries, who still remain, — and with this pause of memory, gratitude and reverence, I own the lapse, the breaches and the blessings too of time, — and pay my humble tribute to the friends who taught and led my childhood and added to its happiness and peace and hopes.

To you, to whom this hour belongs, whose right it is to claim the thought and effort of the occasion, I know I do not need to excuse this moment of delay. Nor indeed do I either think or feel that any cold and formal teaching of the brain, or that any didactic sermonizing — were it ever so faultless or ever so true in its doctrine, style, or logic — would be the service with which I might best illustrate the office of such an anniversary.

At the close of an annual period of academic study, when some are leaving these abodes for new, or for older homes, for duties more solitary, active and responsible; when all are making a rest, making a period or a term, in the progress of life and its education; at this moment, when sensitive natures feel so much; when the hopeful paint so brilliantly the images of all they fancy in what remains to come; I would that I might speak — not circuitously *through* the understanding, but directly *to you*, yourselves.

I know something of what lies unspoken, and but very rarely spoken *to*, in the inmost of your souls. In the clearer and more thoughtful moments of all your lives, I know there are moods of thought and feeling, when duty, when the grand possibilities that are open to us all, when the ideal of a noble life, the visions of a truth and beauty, such as even the instruction of bards cannot tell in word, and such as only saints and heroes have made actual, possess and hold you.

It is to those best moments I wish I had the gift to speak, so that they might not end in the mere luxury of reverie, but might rise up to the solemn beauty of stern and high resolve, so that the dull prose of actual homely cares might not dissolve that poetic charm, leaving only a few tears and vain regrets, half real and half romantic, as the poor remains of what might have been a perpetual feast with the immortals. Those are the hours of your visitation; then it is that the gateways of the celestial and eternal city are opening for you; the winged ones are fluttering around you, and the influx of wisdom and love from the Lord himself, through all these better thoughts and visions, comes in to strengthen, warm and regenerate. Sometimes in books we find the story of our own lives as those lives are told in the hours when life is thus transfigured before us; sometimes in history, sometimes in fiction, when poetry paints a life, the poet himself could imagine but never led. Sometimes in men and women whom we know, we see and recognize traits; and sometimes — but more rarely — characters, filled out and rounded up, which seem to be the originals of our own best aspiration. And, *then*, feeling that what we scarcely dared to *hope* is not only possible to the contemplation, but is already a fact of real life, we are sometimes encouraged by perceiving how possible indeed is a true and noble character; and more often, perhaps, dismayed by the desolate distance at which we halt behind.

Then, too, we come to know (because we *feel* that it is true) that it is not what we *say*, nor what we *do*, but what we *are*, by which we are most truly known to God; by which we are most truly judged by our own examination of ourselves; by which we are felt from the centre to the circumference of each one's sphere.

Character; or what we *are*. That is what colors and gives tone and purpose to what we do and what we say; that speaks in the voice, looks out from under the eye-lids, smiles or curls on the lip, blushes in the cheek, clenches or unbends the hand, flushes or calms the brow.

It is this which makes the plain man look noble, and the proud man mean. It is this which makes some countenances a benediction when they pass, and some visages hard, sour, and insignificant. I want no letter of introduction to accompany a noble man, or a sweet and genuine woman. The certificates are impertinent which testify on paper to what is written on the speaking brow, and lip and eye, and cheek, which veil but do not hide the translucent soul. Do you talk of the sway or influence of some great person; call it, if you please, some powerful leader of a party in the State; some strong-willed, clear-minded leader of a sect; of some woman, who leads the fashion of her town; or better still, directs the tone and quality of social custom there; or better still, is felt in the thought and culture of its circle? Do you tell me that you are not captivated, nor won over to reverence or love either the one or the other of them? And, do you ask, where is the title-deed to this magnificent power, that you do not see it? I tell you that the power and all the power they hold, or ever had, perhaps you yield to as much as any others do. They may be strong, but narrow; real forces in the direction, government, and growth of States and social circles; but *good* only in the absence of those who would be *better*. Or look again, lest you be dazzled by an apparent power, which is not real. There *is* an influence essentially of the man; and so there is an influence only accidental to him.

In the absence of a natural, providential leader, like Moses, like Cæsar, like Washington, people sometimes choose an official leader, who best represents the average of the prejudices and ignorance of all. But when he is chosen, he is recognized only as one of the parts of the great social machine, which *must* be kept in its motion; not as the talismanic name, the brave heart, the clear, sound head, the true, devoted friend of all; the representative of their best thought, their best culture, their highest aim, and their profoundest faith.

The queen-bee is not created by the votes in a ballot-box. She presides because she *is* a *Queen.* She is a centre of an influence as subtle as it is resistless, and as significant and beautiful as it is real and true.

Let who will be Pope, by the suffrages of the Cardinals, wearing the triple crown, scattering formalistic benedictions and pretending to be the Peter of the Church; when · Ignatius Loyola comes, smitten with a burning, quenchless zeal, possessed by his idea, and alive with a faith that sees no mountain too large, no sacrifice too great, — it is *Loyola,* not the Pope, who rules, though he wears no crown. It is *Loyola* who gives success and power, and is the *Rock,* though he does not claim the successorship of *Peter.*

Leo X. may fulminate from the Seven Hills, affect the attributes of him whose vicar he claims to be, may bind and loose on earth, and pretend to bind and loose in Heaven. Kings may bow down, and the Christian world stand in awe of him. But a monk arises, in a distant University of Germany; he is one man against the multitude; a learned and pious man against the mighty spiritual and temporal potentates of the great States of Europe. The prejudices and accumulated opinions of one thousand years stand up behind the vast array of powers and men. But Luther stands almost alone, planted on the truth he saw, and the faith he knew, and the invincible truth, represented and testified, in the person of a man, whose very voice and style and mien were the distinct embodiment of earnest, certain and defiant conviction, vitalizing, informing and creating a *character* equal to the emergency, fitting the man himself to the hour he came, revealed to Rome, to Christendom, and to Humanity, the unconquerable hero of an irresistible and imperishable reform.

Victoria, covered by the imagined majesty with which a loyal people invest a Queen, whose dominions belt the globe, — perhaps quite as worthy as a matron as she is grand by her regal position, — is, to the unsophisticated heart, as she surely must and will be in the long history of the hereafter, a pale and ineffectual fire, when we contrast with her accidental greatness, the Heaven-elected *Florence Nightingale.* *Birth*, and the ordinances of a State, made the one a *British Queen.* CHARACTER made the other — oh, how much more than royal, an almost peerless *woman.* Elizabeth Fry, Mary Ware, Dorothea Dix, and Harriet Ryan, — I name a few conspicuous examples from a catalogue, all more or less illustrious, which your memory will fill up, — such as these are the bright examples which decorate, while they bless humanity of the character I mean.

That greatness which is good, and that goodness which is also great, do not constitute a marble statue, in which one critic may point out the powerful proportions of herculean strength, and another suggest the perfection of Apollo's manly beauty. That character at which I have hinted, but am not vain enough to believe my words can fitly describe, is not a picture in which you may study the beauty of its coloring, the accuracy of its delineation, the truth of its outline, or the harmony of its effect. It is as much more than a statue, — it is as much more than a painting, as Nature is more and better than Art.

CHARACTER, in the sense I mean when I have spoken of these powerful and beautiful persons, is open to the acquisition of us all; not less in the cool sequestered vale than on the giddy heights of conspicuous greatness.

You may achieve it, as well as all they who out of weakness were made strong, of whom the world was not worthy, who through faith have subdued kingdoms, and obtained the promises.

For I have named these only for illustration. The qualities which we admire in the prophetic heart, the cosmopolitan genius, the universal culture and the intensity of thought, will, and feeling, of the Hungarian statesman and orator, Louis Kossuth; the brilliant daring, the lion-hearted independence, the clearness of conception joined to the intrepidity and skill of execution, which have astonished Europe in the exploits of the Italian patriot and hero, Joseph Garibaldi, all, all lie, whether as rudiments of character, or as possibilities of accomplishment, in every man.

I have seen, I think, a heroism as real and as poetic in humble men, who had no history, and hardly claimed to hope for a tombstone or an epitaph. I have heard an eloquence as touching to the heart and as stirring to the blood, as any which ever inspired armies on the eve of battle, or senates in great emergencies of nations; eloquence from as pure fountains of crystal thought and feeling, albeit the men and women who spoke have never had a name in the schools of rhetoric, will never be reported in any printed page. And I have seen a devotedness, as true to high ideals of the purest chivalry, as any I have read of in the books that testify of fame.

I own that I almost lose my patience, and find it hard to maintain the grace of charity, when I hear the croaking of those who with eyes which see nothing but faults, and ears which hear nothing but confusion, are permitted to walk on God's green earth, to enjoy the society of man and the providence of Heaven, and who see no beauty and no good. Bad, indeed, as some men become in the deep selfishness of their cold, inhuman hearts, I have scarcely come to know *one*, who did not reveal some better traits than even his friends had told me of.

No; believe them not.   Be not deceived by the comparisons and contrasts seen in the conditions, opportunities, and original qualities of different men.   Judged by any standard erected here on earth, they may seem to be wide, hopelessly wide, apart. But place your point of observation in the Heavens, where the Infinite One, who knoweth and loveth all, stands and surveys us here; and the infinite distance at which we all are from him, dwarfs all human differences, so that we may begin to comprehend what is meant by seeing as we are seen, and knowing as we are known.

No; and therein is the longing of your better hours after the realization of truth and beauty, after the highest good, in your own lives, a *prophecy* as well as a desire of the heart.   Because, what in the parlance of the world we call greatness, success, prosperity, wealth, power, position, are only the accidents or opportunities, of which noble and genuine men and women avail themselves, when they come to them. These things, which I have called the accidents or opportunities of a man, may shift and scatter like the autumn leaves. They may desert him utterly, and leave him as bare and poor and desolate as Lear. But they have not deprived him of himself, nor of any thing essentially his; not of one real gift, nor one element of his real greatness.

How much finer do we sometimes see the quality of persons show itself, when sudden calamity has unhorsed them and driven them to their feet, — when they are enabled to find in themselves, and to develope openly, the great qualities of patience, resignation, and personal independence; of thrift and economy, of industry and the capacity of usefulness, of cheerful dignity in the face of narrow means and altered circumstances. How much all of us become indebted to those who reveal the fragrance of a character, made more winning, more loving, and more brave and peaceful, by being thrown back upon itself and its trust in God.

It is easy to be grand on great occasions. In an army of 180,000 men, just led by Napoleon for the relief of Italy, how many there were, of each of whom it might have been said as of Murat, *He was the bravest of the brave.* How few, indeed, disclosed in fight the lack of personal, physical courage and endurance, which we recognize as the heroism of the field. In the perilous edge of battle, where it raged the hottest, they poured in streams of thousands and ten thousands, a human torrent, rising, surging, melting, gathering, receding and swelling up again, like a stream encountering the rocks and head-lands that impede its current. The columns stagger and fall before the awful storms of leaden rain and iron hail; and warriors unhorsed, and dead and dying, cover all the ground. For every man who falls another comes, springs to the breach, supplies his place, courts for himself the same caress of death, and in the frenzy of the fight becomes a living miracle of self-forgetfulness, and of the triumphant heart and will of man. The courage of battle is the rule, while cowardice on the field is the comparatively rare exception.

But though I confess to a swelling of the heart, to a quickening of the pulse, when I read the story of such scenes as every battle-field presents, proving the grand capacity of self-abnegation there is in every man; and how men will lose themselves in any cause; and how the intoxication of mere vulgar glory will absorb every passion, even the instinctive love of life, — I confess I perceive that those, too, are occasions when it is easy to be great.

I turn to a poor young man, a conscript of France. He has followed the imperial standard across the Alps, leaving at home a mother straining her weary eyes after the fortunes of her boy. His heart was warm and his hope was high. But the waves of sorrow have overwhelmed him.   Wounded on the field of victory, he is carried bleeding and faint, after hours of unalleviated pain, into a crowded hospital, where by the hands of the regimental surgeon, he who began the day strong and brave, proud in the vigor of his manhood, is left the maimed wreck of what he was. In his dreadful and sickening sense of desolation, the home and the mother return to him.   But he remembers them not to vex himself with unmanly, vain regrets; not to make his torment worse by adding to his fever and distress by useless longings.

No; but he first indites a cheerful letter to the mother, who might hear of his fall, without hearing that his life was spared, and supports her aged and maternal heart by such words as these : " Mother, the surgeon of my regiment has just taken off my leg.   I have always been used to having it, and it was cruel to part ; but, mother, we will not worry about its loss.   You know, when I am at home again, you will *always* have me by your side, to join you at your table." Poor boy! Brave, noble boy! Noble in that beautiful affection which made him cheerful for a mother's sake; noble in that serenity of courage, which, looking aloft, had caught the spirit, if not the formal word, of " Faith, which casts anchor upwards, where storms do never domineer." That was a bravery which outvies the madness of the field.

I doubt not that in the annals of many a New England village there are incidents of as real nobleness and refinement of character as any which decorate the lives of grand, historic personages, less conspic-uous, less demonstrative, perhaps, but in quality and in kind, the same.

> A man that looks on glasse,
>   On it may stay his eye ;
> Or, if he pleaseth, through it passe,
>   And then the heav'n espie.

> All may of thee partake ;
>   Nothing can be so mean,
> Which with his tincture (for thy sake)
>   Will not grow bright and clean.

> A servant with this clause
>   Makes drudgerie divine ;
> Who sweeps a room as for thy laws,
>   Makes that and th' action fine.

And I doubt not the meanness and ignobleness of many, even of those whose advantages of talent and culture had entitled the world to expect of them useful and exemplary lives.

I have endeavored, in these hasty reflections, to encourage you : 1st. To reverence the Good that speaks within you. 2d. To believe in the possibility of a life which shall satisfy the best aspirations. 3d. To recognize all times, places and conditions, as equally real, if less conspicuous opportunities of moral greatness.

And now I pray you to let me, in perhaps a little more practical and simple method, speak in direct application to that most interesting part of this day's audience, for whom the sympathies of the hour are all enlisted. I have avoided, young ladies, the language of didactic morality, of theologic instruction. I have used words of the broadest significance, speaking of human life and hopes, duties and capacities, desiring to transcend all boundaries of opinion and strike home to honest hearts.

I have trusted myself to address the heart of ardent and ingenuous youth, from a standpoint of thought with which I feel sure honest and hopeful minds will sympathize. And, do not mistake me, I am not talking in the sense of romance. I have been paying no tribute to fancy, have not been indulging day-dreams, nor reveries. I believe in character, as a real thing, an essence and a power.

Of all your education, the highest object is to establish *that*. Education is not an accumulation of facts ; it is not a system of philosophy. It is not language, nor mathematics. Education aims to furnish the means and materials by which the mind shall ascertain and cultivate its relations to all truth and all duty. And be sure that you have had but a cramped and unnatural growth, have studied with mistaken views and false aims, if the acquisition of the facts of history, the truths of nature, the results of learning, have not enriched your souls, enlarged your scope of thought, deepened your insight, given you a better hope, a fairer grace and culture of the heart than you had before.

We consult a dictionary; we study a science, we roam through libraries, culling here and there a fact, or a flower of thought. We find what we wish, and we leave behind the books, and care, perhaps, little for them, more. We have mastered the book; and the thought of the writer has passed into the mind and become a part of ourselves. Not so with our acquaintance with a refined, cultivated, educated friend or neighbor. Such a character is always fresh, fragrant and new. It grows with every day; all the experiences enrich it, all the cares of life tend to develope it, all studies enlarge it. Even deprivations and disappointments strike its roots deeper down towards the eternal centre. Conversation feeds it, contemplation and conflict both strengthen it, and the trials of life sanctify it.

Look within, my friends. Judge ye for yourselves whether your idea of the education of the school has thus embraced and filled out your ideal of a womanly life.

Christina, Queen of Sweden, the daughter of the immortal Gustavus Adolphus, herself one of those meteoric persons who seem to have been made for the benefit of biographers and to puzzle honest people, speaking of her own remorseless industry, says, "the men and women who waited on me were quite in despair, for I gave them no rest night nor day." And such was her incessant mental activity that she acquired the reputation of immense learning. She was reputed to have rapidly and thoroughly mastered Greek, Latin, most of the modern languages, history, philosophy, mathematics, geography, astronomy, divinity and moral duties, as interpreted by John Matthias, a pious, earnest man, from Luther's Catechism and the best authors. But, adds one who has sketched her character, the duty of reverencing her mother, the tender, loving wife and faithful widow of the great Gustavus, was not, it would seem, included, for so pained, offended at last, became the disconsolate lady, with the conduct of Christina, that she fled in secret to Denmark, declaring that she preferred begging her bread elsewhere, to the state of queen-mother at her own daughter's court. That she had great capacity, we know, although we would not receive for gospel truth the exaggeration and bombast of the courtier who described her as " born with the head of a Machiavel, the heart of a Titus, the courage of an Alexander, and the eloquence of a Tully."

Her father, lion of the North and bulwark of the Protestant faith, had fallen at the battle of Lutzen, in Upper Saxony. Sweden, thought to have been, by the fall of Gustavus, hurled from her place among the nations, and the cause of scriptural truth, struck down in the person of its most powerful champion, were both deemed to have been saved and restored by the prophetic advice of the veteran Chancellor, Oxenstiern, who proposed the immediate enthronement of Christina, then only six years of age, and her recognition as the Queen of Sweden.

Amid the general joy the baby queen was placed upon the throne of the great Protestant warrior. And Sweden and the faith were declared in her person to have found salvation.

At sixteen years old, she openly presided in the Senate, and a French ambassador says she was "incredibly powerful therein." At eighteen she governed, without any check, as a monarch of absolute power.

But she was imperious, arbitrary, and self-willed; she exhausted all her grand resources of occupation and amusement. At one time the most violent supporter of letters and literary men; at another she forswore them all, insulted and degraded scholars and philosophers with indignities and meanness not to be borne; abused her friends, berated all her sex, betrayed her mission both as a queen and a woman; and in twenty-two years after her ascent to the throne, quitted it in satiety and disgust, abdicated in favor of Charles Augustus, the Crown Prince of Sweden, left the kingdom with her private treasures, recanted the faith of her father and the doctrines of the Reformation, was admitted into the Church of Rome, and, after that, describes her own employment, in a private letter, in terms like these: —

"I eat well, sleep well, study a little, chat, laugh, see French and Italian plays, and pass my time in agreeable dissipation. I hear no sermons, and utterly despise all orators. As Solomon says, all wisdom is vanity; everyone ought to live contentedly, eat, drink, and be merry."

She lived without a conscience, and she halted at no crime.

Such is the outline of the story and life of a great and powerful princess, on whom nature and accidental position had lavished the noblest gifts; on whom the highest hopes of religion and the State reposed; whose vigorous health, commanding abilities, fondness and fitness for labor, and whose opportunities of instruction had enabled her to become celebrated for her acquirements in many of the departments of learning. With many royal qualities, as well as a royal station, she became, at the best, but a splendid ruin.

Elizabeth Gurney (afterwards Mrs. Fry), was on her father's side the daughter of an ancient English family, and was, through her mother, descended from Robert Barclay, the early apologist of Quakerism. John Gurney, her father, was a man of great respectability and large wealth. Her mother was beautiful, gifted and good. Elizabeth was four years old when her family removed from their residence to Earlham Hall, about two miles from Norwich, a stately old mansion, once belonging to the Verulam family, commanding a scene of great natural beauty in a wooded park, by the silver stream of Wensum. Her father not belonging to the class known as *plain* Quakers, and being a rich man, his family were never, in any disciplinary sense, formal or rigid "Friends." She was taught music, dancing, drawing, and other ornamental accomplishments. She was quite a proficient in operatic music, and greatly delighted in the amusement of dancing, in which, by her vivacity and grace, she easily excelled.

She never disclosed any fondness for the toils of study, and seemed to dislike the routine of lesson learning and recitation, gained no celebrity as a scholar, either by any exhibition of native talent, or by any industry in the search of knowledge.

She was conscious of having a keen relish for admiration and light amusements, and naïvely said, after having seen the Prince of Wales at the opera: "I do,

I own, love grand company;" and at another time ingenuously admits, "I do love a piece of scandal."

One morning, in 1804, when Elizabeth Fry was scarcely twenty-four years old, a party of Quaker friends visited the miserable quadrangular enclosure, in Newgate Jail, where some three hundred female prisoners were herded together, in squalor, filth, and all external signs of misery. They were many of them profane, obscene, and drunken. But, without regard to age, or the quality of their offences, and without regard to the fact whether they were convicted felons, or only suspected persons detained for trial, the poor creatures stood there together under one common curse of social outlawry, poverty and shame.

"They are utterly irreclaimable, be assured; sunk in depravity and crime beyond the power of rescue," declared an officer of Newgate, to a suggestion of one of the "Friends," in behalf of these poor sisters of sin and misfortune. The Chris-

tian churches and people of England, —
of that England "whose flag had braved a
thousand years, the battle and the breeze,"
on whose empire the sun never sets, whose
naval and military power, whose commercial influence, and whose literature,
science and jurisprudence, outshone the
splendors of any other land in any age,
and whose church establishment and dis-
senting clergy combined, presented an
array of scholars and divines, unsurpassed
in the history of the Protestant faith,—were
helpless and powerless to give a ray of
hope to the poor and wretched whom the
Master had most especially commanded
them to visit and succor. " Thou dost not
surely mean, that they are beyond the
power and the reach of God?" exclaimed
Elizabeth Fry, in a voice singularly sweet
by nature, and with her peculiarly clear,
thrilling tone.

A few days afterwards the youthful
matron, now in the fulness of her womanhood, tall, fair and graceful, then a "plain

Quaker," but still richly habited in the costume of her sect, reappeared at Newgate, asked to be admitted to the quadrangle and to be left there alone with the female prisoners. Astounded at the request, the Governor and all the officials of Newgate, chaplain included, endeavored to dissuade the beautiful missionary from encountering the disgusting contact, the dangerous and hopeless task. " I am in the hands of God, and in his fear I feel no other." Her character, her social position as a gentlewoman, her persistent firmness, overcame the officials, and she entered. From the words of the Saviour she read aloud out of the open book. The sweet promise, the tender invitations of grace, fell on the ears of women who knew God and Christ only as words with which to intensify a curse, or only as dim memories of a buried hope.

The pathetic tone of that charming voice, and her beautiful countenance, lit up by heavenly love, seemed to make her the embodiment in flesh of the sublime charity she taught.

The tumult of beggary, audacity and folly, which saluted her approach, subsided, as she read. The magnetism of love leaped from her serene and pious heart to theirs. They stay their Babel cries to catch the accents and the words of so much tenderness. The quenchless spark of the Divine was fanned by Heaven's own breath, and warmed in those poor hearts anew. "Hush" (when some slight noise disturbed again the current of her reading), "Hush," exclaimed a woman with glittering eye and fevered cheek, "the angels have lent her their voices."

Six years before, Mrs. Fry, then the gay and beautiful Elizabeth Gurney, listened at Norwich to William Savery, a Quaker preacher from America, who bore earnest and solemn testimony of the dangers that beset those "who wander from the simple, safe path of self-denial." She went home weeping in her carriage. William Savery saw her at her father's home, at Earlham Hall, and pointed her to a future career of usefulness and true nobility in the love of God and her fellowmen.

" Strange, indeed, that it should be said to me that I may prove sight to the blind, speech to the dumb, and feet to the lame. Can it be?" Yes, Elizabeth, and more, far more, than these; thou shalt be soaring *wings* to sinking hearts and heavy-laden souls, bearing them up from the clouds and pestilence of earth to the peace of Heaven.

You know her long and self-denying life, commanding respect and winning love; a bright example of womanhood, by the purity and beauty of a character as simple and unaffected as any poet ever dreamed of in sylvan life, and as steadfast as the rock of truth she stood on. The humble, the poor, and the prisoner, loved her as their friend; the highest in the land gave to her the homage of their unaffected admiration. In the sixty-seventh year of her age, she breathed out her spirit, with a smile on her lips, as if an angel had kissed them, whispering in death: "It is a strife, but I am safe."

Contrast the life and the words of Christina, the proud and talented Swedish queen, with the life, and the peaceful parting words of Elizabeth Fry, and remember the selfishness of the one, and the self-devotion of the other.

The character of Christina was formed on the pattern of a vain-glorious, self-seeking and absorbing egotism; Elizabeth Gurney was recalled in her girlhood to the "*simple, safe path of self-denial*" by the inspiring earnestness of the Quaker preacher.

Whether in the pursuits of learning, of power, of fame or pleasure, Christina was the proud, imperious queen, and the heartless epicurean. Elizabeth conquered her young frivolities, cleared and concentrated her intellectual powers by purifying her heart and reposing her soul on immortality.

There is no mystery in a true and noble
life. " The word is very nigh unto thee.
It is in thy heart." Be true to the highest
good you know; stand fast by the teaching and the warning of your best and
tenderest hours. In the quiet of the study,
in the whirl of social life, in the engross-
ment of daily toils, in the absorption of
domestic cares, in the relations of the fire-
side, of the neighborhood and of society,
still be faithful and true, speaking little of
duty, but doing much. There is a secret
in every soul, between itself and God.
Guard it as the vestal fire.

It is your assurance of usefulness and
peace for ever. In quietness and confidence, with smiling face and cheerful,
hearty voice, pass on from duty to duty,
through all the cares and trials of your lot.
Affect no singularities of speech or style.
Be catholic, charitable, amiable, firm and
free. Forbid no man nor woman. Let
each exorcise sin and slay the adversary in
his own way. Life is too short, and the

field is too white, for debate among the reapers. Forget the words applause and fame. You shall win more than popularity; you shall command the sweet rewards of Love.

VALEDICTORY ADDRESS

TO THE

TWO BRANCHES OF THE LEGISLATURE.

JANUARY 5, 1866.

On retiring from office, Governor Andrew delivered the following address to the General Court of Massachusetts; "the sentiments and logic of which he maintained, without qualification, to the day of his death; and by which he expressed a wish that his title to fame in the history of his country should be determined." Of this memorable scene an eye-witness says: "Who that was present can forget that last day in office? He invited to his rooms a large number of his friends to go in with him and hear the address. There you saw together a remarkable company. There were men and women of all ages; from Levi Lincoln, then eighty-four years of age, to little boys and girls. Side by side were old abolitionists and old conservatives, orthodox men and radicals — those who had never met before in one room in their lives."

VALEDICTORY ADDRESS.

Gentlemen of the Senate and the
House of Representatives : —

THE people of Massachusetts have vindicated alike their intelligence, their patriotism, their will, and their power; both in the cultivation of the arts of Peace, and in the prosecution of just and unavoidable War. At the end of five years of Executive administration, I appear before a Convention of the two Houses of her General Court, in the execution of a final duty.

For nearly all that period, the Commonwealth, as a loyal State of the American Union, has been occupied, within her sphere of co-operation, in helping to maintain, by arms, the power of the nation, the liberties of the people, and the rights of human nature.

Having contributed to the Army and the Navy—including regulars, volunteers, seamen, and marines, men of all arms and officers of all grades, and of the various terms of service—an aggregate of one hundred and fifty-nine thousand one hundred and sixty-five men; and having expended for the war, out of her own Treasury, twenty-seven million seven hundred and five thousand one hundred and nine dollars,—besides the expenditures of her cities and towns, she has maintained, by the unfailing energy and economy of her sons and daughters, her industry and thrift, even in the waste of war. She has paid promptly, and *in gold*, all interest on her bonds,—including the old and the new,—guarding her faith and honor with every public creditor, while still fighting the public enemy; and now, at last, in retiring from her service, I confess the satisfaction of having first seen all of her regiments and batteries, (save two battalions,) returned and mustered out of the Army; and of leaving her treasury provided for, by the fortunate and profitable negotiation of all the permanent loan needed or foreseen — with her financial credit maintained at home and abroad, her public securities unsurpassed, if even equalled, in value in the money market of the world by those of any State or of the Nation.

I have already had the honor to lay before the General Court, by special message to the Senate, a statement of all affairs which demand my own official communication. And it only remains for me, to transfer, at the appropriate moment, the cares, the honors, and the responsibilities of office, to the hands of that eminent and patriotic citizen, on whose public experience and ability the Commonwealth so justly relies.

But, perhaps, before descending, for the last time, from this venerable seat, I may be indulged in some allusion to the broad field of thought and statesmanship, to which the war itself has conducted us.

As I leave the Temple where, humbled by my unworthiness, I have stood so long, like a priest of Israel sprinkling the blood of the holy sacrifice on the altar — I would fain contemplate the solemn and manly duties which remain to us who survive the slain, in honor of their memory and in obedience to God.

The Nation having been ousted by armed Rebellion of its just possession, and the exercise of its constitutional jurisdiction over the territory of the Rebel States, has now at last, by the suppression of the Rebellion, (accomplished by the victories of the national arms over those of the Rebels,) regained possession and restored its own rightful sway.

The Rebels had overthrown the loyal State Governments. They had made war against the Union. The government of each Rebel State had not only withdrawn its allegiance, but had given in its adhesion to *another*, viz., *The Confederate Government*, — a government, not only injurious by its very creation, but hostile to, and in arms against, the Union, asserting and exercising belligerent rights, both on land and sea, and seeking alliances with foreign nations, even demanding the armed intervention of neutral powers.

The pretensions of this " Confederacy " were maintained for some four years, in one of the most extensive, persistent and bloody wars of History. To overcome it and maintain the rights and the very existence of the Union, our National Government was compelled to keep on foot one of the most stupendous military establishments the world has ever known. And probably the same amount of force, naval and military, was never organized and involved in any national controversy.

On both sides there was *war*, with all its incidents, all its claims, its rights and its results.

The States in rebellion tried, under the lead of their new Confederacy, to conquer the Union ; but in the attempt they were themselves conquered.

They did not revert by their rebellion, nor by our conquest, into " Territories." They did not commit suicide. But they rebelled, they went to war; and they were *conquered.*

A " territory " of the United States is a possession, or dependency, of the United States, having none of the distinctive, constitutional attributes of a State. A territory might be in rebellion; but not thereby cease to be a territory. It would be properly described as *a territory in rebellion.* Neither does a State in rebellion cease to be a State. It would be correctly described, *a State in rebellion.* And it would be subject to the proper consequences of rebellion, both direct and incidental, — among which may be that of military government, or supervision, by the nation, determinable only by the nation, at its own just discretion, in the due exercise of the rights of war. The power to put an end to its life is not an attribute of a State of our Union. Nor can the Union put an end to its own life, save by an alteration of the National Constitution, or by suffering such defeat, in war, as to bring it under the jurisdiction of a conqueror. The nation has a vested interest in the life of the individual State. The States have a vested interest in the life of the Union. I do not perceive, therefore, how a State has the power by its own action alone, without the co-operation of the Union, to destroy the continuity of its corporate life. Nor do I perceive how the National Union can by its own action, without the action or omission of the States, destroy the continuity of its own corporate life. It seems to me that the stream of life flows through both State and Nation from a double source; which is a distinguishing element of its vital power. Eccentricity of motion is not death; nor is abnormal action organic change.

The position of the rebel States is fixed by the Constitution, and by the laws, or rights, of war. If they had conquered the

Union, they might have become independent, or whatever else it might have been
stipulated they should become, by the
terms of an ultimate treaty of peace. But
being conquered, they failed in becoming
independent, and they failed in accomplish-
ing anything but their own conquest. They
were still States, — though belligerents
conquered. But they had lost their loyal
organization as States, lost their present
possession of their political and representative power in the Union. Under the Constitution they have no means nor power
of their own to regain it. But the exigency
is provided for by that clause in the Federal Constitution in which the Federal
Government guarantees a republican form
of government to every State. The regular and formal method would be, therefore,
for the National Government to provide
specifically for their re-organization.

The right and duty, however, of the
General Government, under the circumstances of their present case, is not the

single one of re-organizing these disorganized States. The war imposed rights and duties, peculiar to itself, and to the relations and the results of War. The first duty of the Nation is to regain its own *power*. It has already made a great advance in the direction of its power.

If ours were a despotic government, it might even now be thought that it had already accomplished the re-establishment of its power as a government. But, ours being a republican and a popular government, it cannot be affirmed, that the proper power of the government is restored, until a peaceful, loyal and faithful state of mind gains a sufficient ascendancy in the rebel and belligerent States, to enable the Union and loyal citizens everywhere to repose alike on the purpose and the ability of their people, in point of numbers and capacity, to assert, maintain and conduct State Governments, republican in form, loyal in sentiment and character, with safety to themselves and to the national

whole. If the people, or too large a portion of the people, of a given rebel State,
are not willing and able to do this, then
the state of war still exists, or at least, a
condition consequent upon and incidental
thereto exists, which only the exercise on
our part of belligerent rights, or some of
their incidents, can meet or can cure. The
rights of war must continue until the objects of the war have been accomplished,
and the nation recognizes the return of a
state of peace. It is absolutely necessary
then for the Union Government to prescribe some reasonable test of loyalty to
the people of the States in rebellion. It is
necessary to require of them conformity to
those arrangements which the war has
rendered, or proved to be, necessary to the
public peace, and necessary as securities
for the future. As the conquering party,
the National Government has the right to
govern these belligerent States meanwhile,
at its own wise and conscientious discretion, subject: 1st. To the demands of

natural justice, humanity and the usages of civilized nations. 2d. To its duty under the Constitution, to guarantee Republican governments to the States.

But there is no arbiter, save the people of the United States, between the Government of the Union and those States. Therefore the precise things to be done, the precise way to do them, the precise steps to be taken, their order, progress and direction, are all within the discretion of the National Government, in the exercise, both of its belligerent, and its more strictly constitutional, functions,—exercising them according to its own wise, prudent and just discretion. Its duty is not only to restore those States, but also to make sure of a lasting peace, of its own ultimate safety, and the permanent establishment of the rights of all its subjects. To this end, I venture the opinion that the Government of the United States ought to require the people of those States to reform their Constitutions, —

1. Guaranteeing to the people of color, now the wards of the Nation, their civil rights as men and women, on an equality with the white population, by amendments, irrepealable in terms.

2. Regulating the elective franchise according to certain laws of universal application, and not by rules merely arbitrary, capricious and personal.

3. Annulling the ordinances of Secession.

4. Disaffirming the Rebel Debt, and

5. To ratify the anti-slavery amendment of the United States Constitution by their legislatures.

And I would have all these questions, save the fifth — the disposition of which is regulated by the Federal Constitution — put to the vote of the *People* themselves. We should neither be satisfied with the action of the conventions which have been held, nor with what is termed the "loyal vote." We want the *popular* vote. And the rebel vote is better than the loyal vote, if on the right side. If it is not on the right side, then I fear those States are incapable at present of re-organization ; the proper power of the Union Government is not restored ; the people of those States are not yet prepared to assume their original functions with safety to the Union ; and the state of war still exists; for they are contumacious and disobedient to the just demands of the Union, disowning the just conditions precedent to re-organization.

We are desirous of their re-organization, and to end the use of the war power. But I am confident we cannot re-organize political society with any proper security : 1. Unless we let in the *people* to a co-operation, and not merely an arbitrarily selected portion of them. 2. Unless we give those who are, by their intelligence and character, the natural leaders of the people, and who surely will lead them by-and-by, an opportunity to lead them now.

I am aware that it has been a favorite dogma in many quarters, " *No Rebel Vot-*

ers." But — it is impossible in certain States to have *any* voting by white men, if only "loyal men" — *i. e.*, those who continued so, during the rebellion, are permitted to vote. This proposition is so clear that the President adopted the expedient of assuming that those who had not risen above certain civil or military grades in the Rebel public service, and who had neither inherited nor earned more than a certain amount of property, should be deemed and taken to be sufficiently harmless to be intrusted with the suffrage in the work of re-organization. Although there is some reason for assuming that the less conspicuous and less wealthy classes of men had less to do than their more towering neighbors in conducting the States into the Rebellion and through it — still I do not imagine that either wealth or conspicuous position, which are only the accidents of men, or at most, only external incidents, affect the substance of their characters. I think the poorer and less significant men who voted, or fought, for "Southern Independence" had quite as little love for "the Yankees," quite as much prejudice against "the Abolitionists," quite as much contempt for the colored man, and quite as much disloyalty at heart, as their more powerful neighbors.

The true question is, now, not of past disloyalty, but of present loyal purpose. We need not try to disguise the fact, that we have passed through a *great popular revolution.* Everybody in the Rebel States was disloyal, with exceptions too few and too far between to comprise a loyal force, sufficient to constitute the State, even now that the armies of the Rebellion are over-thrown. Do not let us deceive ourselves. The truth is, the public opinion of the white race in the South was in favor of the rebellion. The colored people sympathized with the Union cause. To the extent of their intelligence, they understood that the success of the South meant their continued slavery; that an easy success of the North meant leaving slavery just where we found it; that the *War* meant, if it lasted long enough — their emancipation. The whites went to war and supported the war, because they hoped to succeed in it; since they wanted, or thought they wanted, separation from the Union, or "Southern Independence."   There were, then, three great interests — there were the Southern whites, who as a body, wished for what they called "Southern Independence"; the Southern blacks, who desired emancipation; the people of the "loyal States" who desired to maintain the constitutional rights and the territorial integrity of the Nation.   Some of us in the North had a strong hope, which by the favor of God has not been disappointed, out of our defence of the Union to accomplish the deliverance of our fellow-men in bondage.   But the "*loyal*" *idea* included emancipation, not for its own sake, but for the sake of the Union — if the Union could be saved, or served, by it.   There were many men in the South — besides those known as loyal — who did not like to incur the responsibility of war against the Union; or who did not think the opportune moment had arrived to fight " the North "; or in whose hearts there was "a divided allegiance." But, they were not the positive men. They were, with very few exceptions, not the leading minds, the courageous men, the impressive and powerful characters, — they were not the young and active men. And when the decisive hour came, they went to the wall. No matter what they thought, or how they felt, about it; they could not stand or they would not stand — certainly they did not stand, against the storm. The Revolution either converted them, or swept them off their feet. Their own sons volunteered. They became involved in all the work and in all the consequences of the war. The Southern people — as a people — fought, toiled, endured, and persevered, with a courage, a unanimity and a persistency, not outdone

by any people in any Revolution. There
was never an acre of territory abandoned
to the Union while it could be held by
arms. There was never a Rebel regiment
surrendered to the Union arms until resist-
ance was overcome by force; or a surrender
was compelled by the stress of battle, or
of military strategy. The people of the
South, men and women, soldiers and civil-
ians, volunteers and conscripts, in the army
and at home, followed the fortunes of the
Rebellion and obeyed its leaders, so long
as it had any fortunes or any leaders.
Their young men marched up to the can-
non's mouth, a thousand times, where they
were mowed down like grain by the reapers
when the harvest is ripe. Some men had
the faculty, and the faith in the Rebel
cause, to become its leaders. The others
had the faculty and the faith to follow
them.

All honor to the loyal few! But I do
not regard the distinction between loyal
and disloyal persons of the white race, re-

siding in the South, during the rebellion, as being, for present purposes, a practical distinction. It is even doubtful whether the comparatively loyal few (with certain prominent and honorable exceptions), can be well discriminated from the disloyal mass. And since the President finds himself obliged to let in the great mass of the disloyal, by the very terms of his proclamation of amnesty, to a participation in the business of re-organizing the Rebel States, I am obliged also to confess that I think to make one rule for the richer and higher rebels, and another rule for the poorer and more lowly rebels is impolitic and unphilosophical. I find evidence in the granting of pardons, that such also is the opinion of the President.

When the day arrives, which must surely come, when an amnesty, substantially universal, shall be proclaimed, the leading minds of the South, who by temporary policy and artificial rules had been, for the while, disfranchised, will resume their influence and their sway. The capacity of leadership is a gift, not a device. They whose courage, talents, and will entitle them to lead, will lead. And these men — not then estopped by their own consent or participation, in the business of re-organization — may not be slow to question the validity of great public transactions enacted during their own disfranchisement. If it is asked, in reply, "What can they do?" and "What can come of their discontent?" I answer, that while I do not know just what they can do, nor what may come of it, neither do I know what they may not attempt, nor what they may not accomplish. I only know that we ought to demand, and to secure, the co-operation of the strongest and ablest minds and the natural leaders of opinion in the South. If we cannot gain their support of the just measures needful for the work of safe re-organization, re-organization will be delusive and full of danger.

Why not try them? They are the most

hopeful subjects to deal with, in the very nature of the case. They have the brain and the experience and the education to enable them to understand the exigencies of the present situation. They have the courage, as well as the skill, to lead the people in the direction their judgments point, in spite of their own and the popular prejudice. Weaker men, those of less experience, who have less hold on the public confidence, are comparatively powerless. Is it consistent with reason and our knowledge of human nature, to believe the masses of Southern men able to face about, to turn their backs on those they have trusted and followed, and to adopt the lead of those who have no magnetic hold on their hearts or minds? Re-organization in the South demands the aid of men of great moral courage, who can renounce their own past opinions, and do it boldly; who can comprehend what the work is, and what are the logical consequences of the new situation; men who have interests urging

them to rise to the height of the occasion.
They are not the strong men from whom
weak, vacillating counsels come; nor are
they the great men from whom come counsels born of prejudices and follies, having
their root in an institution they know to
be dead, and buried beyond the hope of
resurrection.

Has it never occurred to us all, that we
are now proposing the most wonderful and
unprecedented of human transactions?
The conquering government, at the close
of a great war, is about restoring to the
conquered rebels not only their local governments in the States, but their representative share in the general government of
the country!   They are, in their States, to
govern themselves as they did before the
rebellion.   The conquered rebels are, in
the Union, to help govern and control the
conquering loyalists!!   These being the
privileges which they are to enjoy, when
re-organization becomes complete, I declare that I know not any safeguard, pre-

caution, or act of prudence, which wise statesmanship might not recognize to be reasonable and just. If we have no right to demand guarantees for the future; if we have no right to insist upon significant acts of loyal submission from the rebel leaders themselves; if we have no right to demand the positive, popular vote in favor of the guarantees we need; if we may not stipulate for the recognition of the just rights of the slaves, whom, in the act of suppressing the rebellion, we converted from slaves into freemen, then I declare that we had no right to emancipate the slaves, nor to suppress the rebellion.

It may be asked: Why not demand the suffrage for colored men, in season for their vote in the business of re-organization? My answer is — I assume that the colored men are in favor of those measures which the Union needs to have adopted. But it would be idle to re-organize those States by the colored vote. If the popular vote of the white race is not to be had in favor of the guarantees justly required, then I am in favor of holding on — just where we now are. I am not in favor of a surrender of the present rights of the Union to a struggle between a white minority aided by the freedmen on the one hand, against a majority of the white race on the other. I would not consent, having rescued those States by arms from secession and rebellion, to turn them over to anarchy and chaos. I have, however, no doubt — none whatever — of our *right* to stipulate for colored suffrage. The question is one of statesmanship, not a question of constitutional limitation.

If it is urged that the suffrage question is one peculiarly for the States, I reply: so also that of the abolition of slavery ordinarily would have been. But we are not now deciding what a loyal State, acting in its constitutional sphere, and in its normal relations to the Union, may do; but what a rebel, belligerent, conquered State must do, in order to be re-organized and to get back into those relations. And in deciding this, I must repeat that we are to be governed only by Justice, Humanity, the Public Safety, and our duty to re-organize those conquered, belligerent States, as we can and when we can, consistently therewith.

In dealing with those States, with a view to fulfilling the national guarantee of a republican form of government, it is plain, since the nation is called upon to re-organize government, where no loyal republican State Government is in existence, that it must, of absolute necessity, deal directly with the *People* themselves. If a State government were menaced and in danger of subversion, then the nation would be called upon to aid the existing government of the State in sustaining itself against the impending danger. But the present case is a different one. The State Government was subverted in each rebel State more than four years ago. The State, in its corporate capacity, went into rebellion; and as long as it had the power, waged

and maintained against the nation rebel-
lious war. There is no government in
them to deal with. But there are the people. It is to the people we must go. It
is through their people alone, and it is in
their primary capacity alone, as people,
unorganized and without a government,
that the nation is capable now of dealing
with them at all. And, therefore, the government of the nation is obliged, by the
sheer necessity of the case, to know who
are the people of the State, in the sense of
the National Constitution, in order to know
how to reach them. Congress, discerning
new people, with new rights, and new
duties and new interests (of the nation itself even), springing from them, may right-
fully stipulate in their behalf. If Congress
perceives that it cannot fulfil its guarantee
to all the people of a State, without such a
stipulation, then it not only may, but it
ought to, require and secure it. The guarantee is one concerning *all*, not merely a
part of the *People*. And, though the gov-

ernment of a State might be of republican form, and yet not enfranchise its colored citizens; still the substance and equity of the guarantee would be violated, if, in addition to their non-enfranchisement, the colored people should be compelled to share the burdens of a State government, the benefits of which would enure to other classes, — to their own exclusion. A republican form of government is not of necessity just and good. Nor is another form, of necessity, unjust and bad. A monarch may be humane, thoughtful and just to every class and to every man. A republic may be inhumane, regardless of, and unjust to, some of its subjects. Our National government and most of the State governments were so, to those whom they treated as slaves, or whose servitude they aggravated by their legislation in the interest of Slavery. The Nation cannot hereafter pretend that it has kept its promise and fulfilled its guarantee, when it shall have only organized governments of republican *form*, unless it can look all the *people* in the face, and declare that it has kept its promise with them all. The voting class alone — those who possessed the franchise under the State Constitutions — were not the *People*. They never were THE PEOPLE. They are not now. They were simply the *Trustees* of a certain power, for the benefit of *all* the people, and not merely for their own advantage. The nation does not fulfil its guarantee by dealing with them alone. It may deal through them, with the people. It may accept their action as satisfactory, in its discretion. But, no matter who may be the agents, through whom the nation reaches and deals with the people, that guaranty of the National Constitution is fatally violated, unless the nation secures to *all the people* of those disorganized States the substantial benefits and advantages of A GOVERNMENT. We cannot hide behind a *word*. We cannot be content with the "*form*." The *substance* bargained for is a *Government.* The "form" is also bargained for, but that is only an incident. The people, and all the people alike, must have and enjoy the benefits and advantages of a *government*, for the common good, the just and equal protection of each and all.

But, What of the policy of the President? I am not able to consider his future policy. It is undisclosed. He seems to me to have left to Congress alone the questions controlling the conditions on which the rebel States shall resume their representative power in the Federal Government. It was not incumbent on the President to do otherwise. He naturally leaves the duty of theoretical reasoning to those whose responsibility it is to reach the just practical conclusion. Thus far the President has simply used, according to his proper discretion, the power of commander-in-chief. What method he should observe was a question of discretion; in the absence of any positive law, to be answered by himself. He might have assumed, in

the absence of positive law — during the
process of re-organization — purely military methods. Had that been needful, it
would have been appropriate. If not necessary, then it would have been unjust and
injurious. It is not just to oppress even
an enemy, merely because we have the
power. In a case like the present, it would
be extremely impolitic, and injurious to
the nation itself. Bear in mind, ours is not
a conquest by barbarians, nor by despots;
but by Christians and republicans. The
commander-in-chief was bound to govern
with a view to promoting the true restora-
tion of the *power* of the Union, as I attempted to describe it in the beginning of
this address; not merely with a view to
the present, immediate control of the daily
conduct of the people. He deemed it wise,
therefore, to resort to the democratic principle, to use the analogies of republicanism
and of constitutional liberty. He had the
power to govern through magistrates, under
military or under civil titles. He could

employ the agencies of popular and of representative assemblies. Their authority has its source, however, in his own war powers as commander-in-chief. If the peace of society, the rights of the government, and of all its subjects, are duly maintained, then the method may justify itself by its success as well as its intention. If he has assisted the people to re-organize their legislatures, and to re-establish the machinery of local State government; though his method may be less regular than if an act of Congress had prescribed it, still, it has permitted the people to feel their way back into the works and ways of loyalty, to exhibit their temper of mind, and to " show their hands." Was it not better for the cause of free government, of civil liberty, to incur the risk of error in that direction, than of error in the opposite one? It has proved that the national government is not drunk with power; that its four years' exercise of the dangerous rights of war has not affected its brain. It has shown that the danger of despotic central-ism, or of central despotism, is safely over.

Meanwhile, notwithstanding the trans-mission of the seals to State magistrates chosen by vote in the States themselves; notwithstanding the inauguration, in fact, of local legislatures, the powers of war re-main. The commander-in-chief has not abdicated. His generals continue in the field. They still exercise military func-tions, according to the belligerent rights of the nation. What the commander-in-chief may hereafter do, whether less or more, depends, I presume, in great measure on what the people of the rebel States may do or forbear doing. I assume that, until the executive and legislative de-partments of the national governments shall have reached the *united* conclusion that the objects of the *war* have been fully accomplished, the national declaration of *peace* is not, and cannot be made.

The proceedings already had, are only certain acts in the great drama of Re-

organization. They do not go for nothing; they were not unnecessary; nor do
I approach them with criticism. But they
are not the whole drama. Other acts are
required for its completion. What they
shall be, depends in part on the wisdom of
Congress to determine.

The doctrine of the President that — in
the steps preliminary to re-organizing a
State which is not, and has not been theo-
retically cut off from the Union — he must
recognize its own organic law, antecedent
to the rebellion, need not be contested. I
adhere, quite as strictly as he, to the logical consequences of that doctrine. I agree
that the Rebel States ought to come back
again into the exercise of their State functions and the enjoyment of their representative power — by the action and by the
votes, of the same class of persons, namely,
the same body of voters, or tenants of
political rights and privileges, by the votes,
action or submission of whom, those States
were carried into the rebellion.

But, yet, it may be, at the same time, needful and proper, in the sense of wise statesmanship, to require of them the amplification of certain privileges, the recognition of certain rights, the establishment of certain institutions, the re-distribution even of political power — to be by them accorded and executed through constitutional amendments, or otherwise — as elements of acceptable re-organization; and as necessary to the re-adjustment of political society in harmony with the new relations, and the new basis of universal freedom, resulting from the Rebellion itself. If these things are found to be required by wise statesmanship, then the right to exact them, as conditions of restoring those States to the enjoyment of their normal functions, is to be found, just where the Nation found the right to crush the Rebellion and the incidental right of emancipating Slaves.

Now, distinctions between men, as to their rights, purely arbitrary, and not founded in reason, nor in the nature of things, are not wise, statesmanlike, nor " Republican," in the constitutional sense. If they ever are wise and statesmanlike, they become so, only where oligarchies, privileged orders and hereditary aristocracies are wise and expedient.

There are two kinds of Republican government, however, known to political science, viz.: Aristocratic Republics and Democratic Republics, or those in which the government resides with a few persons, or with a privileged body, and those in which it is the government of the People. I cannot doubt that nearly all men are prepared to admit that our governments—both State and National—are constitutionally democratic, representative republics. That theory of government is expressly set forth in the Declaration of Independence. The popular theory of government is again declared in the preamble to the Federal Constitution. The Federal government is elaborately con-

structed according to the theory of popular and representative government, and
against the aristocratic theory, in its
distinguishing features.   And, in divers
places, the Federal Constitution, in set
terms, presupposes the democratic and
representative character of the governments of the States; for examples, by
assuming that they have legislatures, that
their legislatures are composed of more
than one body, and by aiming to prevent
even all appearance of aristocratic form,
by prohibiting the States from granting
any title of nobility.   In his recent message to Congress, President JOHNSON
affirms "the great distinguishing principle
of the recognition of the *rights of man*,"
as the fundamental idea, in all our governments.   "The American system," he adds,
in the same paragraph, "rests on the asser-
tion of the *equal right* of every man to life,
liberty and the pursuit of happiness, to
freedom of conscience, to the culture and
exercise of all his faculties."

But, is it pretended that the idea of a government of the People, and for the People, in the American sense, is inclusive of the white race only, or is exclusive of men of African descent? On what ground can the position rest?

The citizenship of free men of color, even in those States where no provision of law seemed to include them in the category of voters, has been frequently demonstrated, not only as a legal right, but as a right asserted and enjoyed.

Nay more; both under the confederation, and in the time of the adoption of the Constitution of the United States, all free native born inhabitants of the States of New Hampshire, Massachusetts, New York, New Jersey, and North Carolina, though descended from African slaves, were not only citizens of those States, but such of them as had the other necessary qualifications, possessed the franchise of Electors on equal terms with other citizens. And even Virginia declares, in her ancient

Bill of Rights, "that all men having sufficient evidence of permanent common interest with, and attachment to the community, have the right of suffrage." Wherever free colored men were recognized as free citizens or subjects, but were, nevertheless, not fully enfranchised, I think the explanation is found, not in the fact of their mere color nor of their antecedent servitude, but in the idea of their possible lapse into servitude again — of which condition their color was a badge and a continuing presumption. The policy of some States seems to have demanded that Slavery should be the prevailing condition of all their inhabitants of African descent. In those States, the possession of freedom by a colored man has therefore been treated as if that condition was only exceptional and transient. But, wherever the policy and legislation of a State were originally dictated by men who saw through the confusion of ideas occasioned by the presence of Slavery, there we are

enabled to discern the evidence of an un-
clouded purpose (with which the American
mind always intended to be consistent),
viz.: *The maintenance of equality between
free citizens concerning civil* RIGHTS, *and
the distribution of* PRIVILEGES, *according to
capacity and desert, and not according to
the accidents of birth.* And now that
Slavery has been rendered for ever impossible within any State or Territory of
the Union, by framing the great natural
law of Universal Freedom into the organic
Law of the Union, all the ancient disa-
bilities which Slavery had made apparently attendant on African descent, must
disappear.

Whatever may be the rules regulating
the distribution of political power among
free citizens, in the organization of such a
republican government as that guaranteed
by the National Constitution, *descent* is
neither the evidence of right, nor the
ground of disfranchisement.

The selection of a fraction or class, of

the great body of freemen in the Civil
State, to be permanently invested with its
entire political power — (selected by mere
human predestination, irrespective of merit)
— that power to be incommunicable to the
freemen of another class — the two classes,
of rulers and ruled, governors and governed, to be determined by the accident of
birth, and all the consequences of that accident to descend by generation to their
children — seems to me to be the establishment of an hereditary aristocracy of
birth, the creation of a privileged order,
inconsistent both with the substance and
the essential form of American republicanism, unstatesmanlike and unwise; and (in
the rebel States), in every sense, dangerous
and unjust.

To demand a certain qualification of
intelligence is eminently safe, and consists
with the interests and rights of all. It
is as reasonable as to require a certain
maturity of age. They who are the representatives of the political power of

society, acting not only for themselves, but also for the women and children, who too belong to it; representing the interests of the wives, mothers, sisters, daughters, infant sons, and the posterity of us all, ought to constitute an audience reasonably competent to hear. And, since the congregation of American Voters is numbered by millions, and covers a continent, it cannot hear with its ears all that it needs to know; but must learn intelligently much that it needs to know, through the printed page and by means of its eyes. The protection of the mass of men against the deceptions of local. demagogues, and against their own prejudices hereafter — as well as the common safety — calls for the requirement of the capacity to read the mother tongue, as a condition of coming for the first time to the ballot-box. Let this be required at the South, and immediately the whole Southern community will be aroused to the absolute necessity of demanding free schools and popular education. These are, more than all things else, to be coveted, both for the preservation of public liberty, and for the temporal salvation of the toiling masses, of our own Saxon and Norman blood, whom alike with the African slave, the oppression of ages has involved in a common disaster.

I think the wisest and most intelligent persons in the South are not ignorant of the importance of raising the standard of intelligence among voters; nor of extending the right to vote, so as to include those who are of competent intellect, notwithstanding the recent disability of color. There is evidence that they are not unwilling to act consistently with the understanding, example, and constitutional precedents of the fathers of the Republic; consistently with the ancient practice of the States, coeval with the organic law of the nation, established by the very men who made that law, who used and adopted the very phrase, "a republican form of government," of the meaning of which their own practice was a contemporary interpretation. But if the conquering power of the nation, if the victorious arm of the Union is paralyzed; if the federal government, standing behind the ramparts of defensive war, wielding its weapons, both of offence in the hour of struggle, and of diplomacy in the hour of triumph, is utterly powerless to stipulate for the execution of this condition; then I confess I do not know how the best and wisest in the South will be enabled, deserted and alone, to stand up on its behalf, against the jealousy of ignorance and the traditions of prejudice.

If the measures I have attempted to delineate are found to be impracticable, then Congress has still the right to refuse to the Rebel States re-admission to the enjoyment of their representative power, until amendments to the *Federal Constitution* shall have been obtained adequate to the exigency. Nor can the people of the rebel States object to the delay. They voluntarily withdrew from Congress; they themselves elected the attitude of disunion. They broke the agreements of the constitution : not we. They chose their own time, opportunity and occasion to make war on the Nation, and to repudiate the Union. They certainly cannot now dictate to us the time nor the terms. Again, I repeat, the just discretion of the nation — exercised in good faith towards all — must govern.

The Federal Union was formed, first of all, "*to establish justice.*" "JUSTICE," in the language of statesmen and of jurists, has had a definition, for more than two thousand years, exact, perfect, and well understood.

It is found in the Institutes of Justinian, —

"Constans et perpetua voluntas, jus suum cuique tribuendi."

"The constant and perpetual will to secure TO EVERY MAN HIS OWN RIGHT."

I believe I have shown that under our federal Constitution, —

1. All the people of the rebel States must share in the benefits to be derived from the execution of the national guarantee of republican governments.

2. That *our* "republican form of government" demands "*The maintenance of equality between free citizens concerning civil* RIGHTS, *and the distribution of* PRIVILEGES, *according to capacity and desert, and not according to the accidents of birth.*"

3. That people "of African descent," not less than people of the white race, are included within the category of free subjects and citizens of the United States.

4. That, in the distribution of political power, under our form of government, "DESCENT *is neither the evidence of right, nor the ground of disfranchisement,*" so that

5. The disfranchisement of free citizens, for the cause of "*descent,*" or for any reason other than lawful disqualification, as by

non-residence, immaturity, crime, or want of intelligence, violates their constitutional rights.

6. That, in executing our national guarantee of republican government to the people of the rebel States, we must secure the constitutional, civic liberties and franchises of all the people.

7. That we have *no right* to omit to secure to the new citizens, made free by the Union, in war, their equality of rights before the law, and their franchises of every sort — including the electoral franchise — according to laws and regulations, of universal, and not of unequal and capricious, application.

We have no right to evade our own duty. We must not, by substituting a new basis for the apportionment of representatives in Congress, give up the just rights of these citizens. Increasing the proportion of the political power of the loyal States, at the expense of the disloyal States, by adopting their relative numbers of *legal voters*, instead of their relative *populations* — while it might punish some States for not according the suffrage to colored men — would not be justice to the colored citizen. For *justice* demands, "*for every man* HIS OWN *right.*"

Will it be said that, by such means, we shall strengthen our own power in the loyal States, to protect the colored people in the South? If we will not yield to them *justice* now, on what ground do we expect grace to give them "*protection*" hereafter?

You will have compromised for a consideration — paid in an increase of your own political power — your right to urge their voluntary enfranchisement on the white men of the South. You will have bribed all the elements of political selfishness, in the whole country, to combine against negro enfranchisement. The States of the rebellion will have no less power than ever in the Senate. And the men who hold the privilege of electing representatives to the lower house, will retain their privilege.   For the sake of doubling the delegation from South Carolina, do you suppose the monopoly of choosing three members would be surrendered by the whites, giving to the colored men the chance to choose six?   Nay:— Would the monopolists gain any thing by according the suffrage to the colored man ; if they could themselves only retain the power to dictate three representatives, and the colored people should dictate the selection of the other three?

The scheme to substitute legal voters, instead of population, as the basis of representation in Congress, will prove a delusion and a snare.   By diminishing the representative power of the Southern States, in favor of other States, you will not increase Southern love for the Union. Nor, while Connecticut and Wisconsin refuse the suffrage to men of color, will you be able to convince the South that your amendment was dictated by political principle, and not by political cupidity. You will not diminish any honest appre-, hension at extending the suffrage, but you will inflame every prejudice, and aggravate discontent. Meanwhile, the disfranchised freedman, hated by some because he is black, contemned by some because he has been a slave, feared by some because of the antagonisms of society, is condemned to the condition of a hopeless pariah of a merciless civilization. *In* the community, he is not *of* it. He neither belongs to a master, nor to society. Bodily present in the midst of the society composing the State, he adds nothing to its weight in the political balance of the nation; and therefore, he stands in the way, occupies the room and takes the place, which might be enjoyed as opportunities by a white immigrant, who would contribute by his presence to its representative power. Your policy would inflame animosity and aggravate oppression, for at least the lifetime of a generation, before it would open the door to enfranchisement.

Civil society is not an aggregation of individuals. According to the order of nature, and of the Divine economy, it is an aggregation of families.

The adult males of the family *vote;* because the welfare of the women and children of the family is identical with theirs; and it is intrusted to their affection and fidelity, whether at the ballot-box or on the battle-field. But, while the voting men of a given community represent the welfare of its women and children, they do not represent that of another community. The men, women and children of Massachusetts, are alike concerned in the ideas and interests of Massachusetts. But, the very theory of representation implies that the ideas and interests of one State are not identical with those of another. On what ground, then, can a State on the Pacific, or the Ohio, gain preponderance in Congress over New Jersey or Massachusetts by reason of its greater number of *males*, while it may have even a less number of *people?* The halls of legislation are the arenas of debate, not of muscular prowess. The intelligence, the opinions, the wishes, and the influence of women, social and domestic, stand for something — for much — in the public affairs of civilized and refined society. I deny the just right of the Government to banish woman from the count. She may not vote, but she thinks; she persuades her husband; she instructs her son. And, through them, at least, she has a right to be heard in the government. Her existence, and the existence of her children, are to be considered in the State.

No matter who changes; let Massachusetts, at least, stand by all the fundamental principles of free, constitutional, republican government.

The President is the tribune of the People. Let him be chosen directly by the popular election. The Senate represents the reserved rights and the equality of the States. Let the Senators continue to be chosen by the Legislatures of the States. The House represents the opinions, interests, and the equality of the *People* of each and every State. Let the people of the respective States elect their representatives, in numbers proportional to the numbers of their people. And let the legal qualifications of the voters, in the election of President, Vice-President, and Representatives in Congress, be fixed by a uniform, equal, democratic, constitutional rule, of universal application. Let this franchise be enjoyed "*according to capacity and desert, and not according to the accidents of birth.*"

Congress may, and ought, to initiate an amendment granting the right to vote for President, Vice-President and Representatives in Congress, to colored men, in all the States, being citizens and able to read, who would by the laws of the States where they reside, be competent to vote if they

were white. Without disfranchising existing voters, it should apply the qualification
to white men also. And, the amendment
ought to leave the election of President
and Vice-President directly in the hands of
the People, without the intervention of
electoral colleges. Then the poorest, humblest and most despised men, being citizens and competent to read, and thus
competent, with reasonable intelligence,
to represent others, would find audience
through the ballot-box. The President,
who is the Grand Tribune of all the People, and the direct delegates of the People
in the popular branch of the National
Legislature, would feel their influence.
This amendment would give efficiency to
the one already adopted, abolishing Slavery
throughout the Union. The two amendments taken together, would practically
accomplish, or enable Congress to fulfil,
the whole duty of the nation to those who
are now its dependent wards.

I am satisfied that the mass of thinking

men at the South accept the present condition of things in good faith; and I am
also satisfied that with the support of a
firm policy from the President and Congress, in aid of the efforts of their good
faith, and with the help of a conciliatory
and generous disposition on the part of the
North — especially on the part of those
States most identified with the plan of
emancipation — the measures needed for
permanent and universal welfare can
surely be obtained.   There ought now to
be *a vigorous prosecution of the Peace,* —
just as vigorous as our recent prosecution
of the War. We ought to extend our
hands with cordial good-will to meet the
proffered hands of the South; demanding
no attitude of humiliation from any; inflicting no acts of humiliation upon any;
respecting the feelings of the conquered —
notwithstanding the question of right and
wrong, between the parties belligerent.
We ought, by all the means and instrumentalities of peace, and by all the thrifty

methods of industry ; by all the re-creative agencies of education and religion, to help rebuild the waste places, and restore order, society, prosperity. Without industry and business there can be no progress. In their absence, civilized man even recedes towards barbarism. Let Massachusetts bear in mind the not unnatural suspicion which the past has engendered. I trust she is able, filled with emotions of boundless joy, and gratitude to Almighty God, who has given such Victory and such Honor to the Right, to exercise faith in his goodness, without vain glory, and to exercise charity, without weakness, towards those who have held the attitude of her enemies.

The offence of War has met its appropriate punishment by the hand of *War*.

In this hour of Triumph, honor and religion alike forbid one act, one word, of vengeance or resentment. Patriotism and Christianity unite the arguments of earthly welfare, and the motives of Heavenly inspiration, to persuade us to put off all jealousy and all fear, and to move forward as citizens and as men, in the work of social and economic re-organization — each one doing with his might whatever his hand findeth to do.

We might wish it were possible for Massachusetts justly to avoid her part in the work of *political* re-organization. But, in spite of whatever misunderstanding of her purpose or character, she must abide her destiny. She is a part of the Nation. The Nation, for its own ends, and its own advantage, as a measure of war, took out of the hands of the masters their slaves. It holds them, therefore, in its hands, as freedmen. It must place them somewhere. It must dispose of them somehow. It cannot delegate the trust. It has no right to drop them, to desert them. For by its own voluntary act, it assumed their guardianship, and all its attendant responsibilities, before the present generation, and all the coming generations, of mankind. I know not how well, nor how ill, they might be treated by the people of the States where they reside. I only know that there is a point beyond which the Nation has no right to incur any hazard. And while the fidelity of the Nation need not abridge the humanity of the States ; on the other hand our confidence in those States cannot be pleaded before the bar of God, nor of history, in defence of any neglect of our own duty.

Let their people remember that Massachusetts has never deceived them. To her ideas of duty and her theory of the Government, she has been faithful. If they were ever misled or betrayed by others into the snare of attempted secession, and the risks of war, her trumpet at least gave no uncertain sound. She has fulfilled her engagements in the past, and she intends to fulfil them in the future. She knows that the re-organization of the States in rebellion carries with it consequences, which come home to the firesides and the

consciences of her own children. For, as
citizens of the Union, they become liable
to assume the defence of those governments, when re-organized, against every
menace, whether of foreign invasion or of
domestic violence. Her bayonets may be
invoked to put down insurgents of whatever color; and whatever the cause,
whether rightful or wrongful, which may
have moved their discontent. And, when
they are called for, they will march. If
she were capable of evading her duty now,
she would be capable of violating her obligations hereafter. If she is anxious to
prevent grave errors, it is because she
appreciates, from her past experience, the
danger of admitting such errors into the
structure of government. She is watchful
against them now, because in the sincere
fidelity of her purpose, she is made keenly
alive to the duties of the present, by con-
templating the inevitable responsibilities
of the future.

In sympathy with the heart and hope of

the nation, she will abide by her faith. Undisturbed by the impatient, undismayed by delay, "with malice towards none, with charity for all; with firmness in the right, as God gives us to see the right," she will persevere. Impartial, democratic, constitutional liberty is invincible. The rights of human nature are sacred; maintained by confessors, and heroes, and martyrs; reposing on the sure foundation of the commandments of GOD.

> " Through plots and counterplots ;
> Through gain and loss ; through glory and disgrace ;
> Along the plains where passionate Discord rears
> Eternal Babel ; still the holy stream
> Of *human happiness* glides on !
>
> .   .   .   .
>
> There is ONE above
> Sways the harmonious mystery of the world."

Gentlemen : — For all the favors, unmerited and unmeasured, which I have enjoyed from the people of Massachusetts; from the councillors, magistrates and officers by whom I have been surrounded in the government; and from the members

of five successive Legislatures; there
is no return in my power to render, but
the sincere acknowledgments of a grateful heart.

University Press: John Wilson & Son, Cambridge.